SOUL SAVER

Sherrie Lowe

Published in 2024 by FeedARead.com Publishing
– Arts Council funded

First Edition

A CIP catalogue record for this title is available from the British Library.

Formatted by The Book Khaleesi

Other Books by Sherrie Lowe

MEMOIRS

Shadow Across the Sun: A Memoir

Better or Dead: More Memoirs

My Furry Loves

NOVELS

Song of the Phoenix

The Author, The Gardener and The Woman What Does

Angel Breaths

Over A Spitfire

Over A Spitfire II: The Sequel

Whisper to Me

WILLOWS DIP SERIES

A Lapse of Sanity - Book 1

After the Solstice - Book 2: The Sequel

Free Flight - Book 3

A Treasure Lost - Book 4

Not Reported Missing – Book 5

Don't Cough on Me – Book 6

COLLECTIONS

Sonnets

Neighbourhood Watching – Willows Dip Shorts

The Journey

Just A Moment

A Treasury of Diverse Tales

SHORT STORY

Love and Roses

Acknowledgements

To The Book Khaleesi for their usual superb formatting and making a professional job of my book.

To feedaread.com for the paperback edition and Amazon for the ebook format.

To my childhood friend who wishes to remain anonymous but she knows who she is, for sharing her church events and services, saving me her newsletters and for the lovely gifts that kept appearing in the post.

All have enriched this story.

To all those I love
Forever in my soul.

CHAPTER 1

June 2023

The Reverend Steven Oswald, vicar of St Luke's parish church in the heart of Willows Dip, sat at his desk in the vicarage adjacent to the church, chewing his pen, staring at the laptop screen, planning the funeral of a parishioner, Mr Bernard Wilshaw, a lonely sixty five year old who had taken his own life.

Steve sighed as he felt he'd failed Bernard. It was his calling to save a soul in distress but this one hadn't shown on his radar. Why? How had he not noticed the man was in emotional turmoil? Bernard didn't live in the heart of Willows Dip, the lanes, the more quaint part of the village, nor on the modern housing estates surrounding it but just on the outskirts in a more affluent cul-de-sac, Regent Grove.

How remiss of him to fold it into his subconscious that just because some of his parishioners had a comfortable lifestyle and were financially secure, that they weren't troubled spiritually or emotionally, as Bernard must have been. He'd lost his wife to cancer some years earlier and his only companion now was their cat, which had been rehomed. There was a younger brother, Frank, Steve had been informed by Jack Adams the young local police officer, and Frank's family, but Bernard and his wife had no children. He needed to make an appointment to meet with Frank to sort out details and family wishes. He looked up at the clock on the wall. 11.15. On impulse he decided to drive round to the house. For what reason he had no tangible answer, there'd be no-one there, just to get a feel of the place, or more so its deceased occupant. Shutting down the laptop, grabbing keys and phone he headed for his trusty but ageing BMW.

Turning into Regent Grove he couldn't help but feel a pang of the deadly sin envy at the beautiful four and five bedroomed homes with their expanses of manicured emerald green lawns bordered by colourful flower beds or sculpted topiary. He quashed the sin as the demon danced before his eyes and focussed his mind on the task in hand feeling another sin – guilt – rise up, that he should have visited before and offered succour to a suffering human being. Well guilt wasn't strictly a sin was it. Pull yourself together man and get on with it.

He found the house, this lawn now in need of a trim, which seemed a pity because the look of the garden was one of neatness, someone who tended his plants. A couple of hanging baskets hung at the front door, which were surprisingly still alive, even though it was several weeks since Bernard's death. There'd had to be an inquest before the body could be released for the funeral because it had been an unexplained death.

He locked the car and walked up the path. It felt intrusive in a way, knowing there was no-one there and not really knowing why he'd come other than on impulse but he was here now so might as well see it through. He fought the ridiculous instinct to knock on the door and almost laughed at himself as he ran his fingers through his dark hair with its silver threads as the wind blew it in his eyes. There was a wrought iron gate leading to the back and he peered through to the garden. Again it would have been a well kept plot and he could imagine it would have been a pleasant place to sit on warm spring days enjoying the birdsong; the solitude.

Well, solitude was a matter of opinion. It could be solitude or it could be loneliness. Solitude was pleasant; loneliness put a completely different complexion on the matter. He was no stranger to either himself. Not since Lisa, his ex wife ran off with a work colleague leaving him and their twin boys, both now left home and living their own lives but it had been difficult to put them through university as a single parent whilst having his own vocation.

"I'm sorry Steve it just happened. You're a good person. It's not you it's me..." and all that bullshit she'd come out with. In the end he'd just wanted her gone, couldn't bear to look at her thinking of her with *him*. Images tortured him. He was done with women. He'd thought she was his soul mate. How could God do this to him when he'd lived a good life spreading His word? He'd almost lost his faith, but not quite, that grain, that tiny thread had kept him going and he'd survived, but if he ever looked at another woman again it would be too soon.

"There's no-one in," came a female voice from the property next door. "It's empty."

His hackles were up immediately and he fought the impulse to say, 'I know that I'm not dumb,' but instead he answered politely, "I know, I just called to see if there was any family here."

"None, well not living here. He had a brother, Frank who used to visit him but he was pretty much a loner since his wife died. I'm Lavinia by the way, Vicar," she added, noticing the dog collar.

"Steve," he replied.

"I've been keeping an eye on the place, watering his hanging baskets, it seemed a shame to let them die. He was always so particular about his garden."

"Yes I can tell it had been well looked after."

She was quite attractive he supposed. Mid fifties – his age – dark hair, pleasantly rounded. When the breeze blew in his direction he caught a hint of her perfume, light and floral. She looked vaguely familiar.

"Any news of when the funeral will be?"

"Not yet. That's partly why I came, to get a feel of his home."

"Ah, I see. Well if there's anything I can help you with feel free to call, either here or I own the florist on the main road outside Willows Dip, 'Say it with Flowers.' You can find me there."

"Oh yes I know it. Right I must be off."

"Nice talking to you."

"You too."

Ha you too! He wouldn't be calling on her or going into her shop – that's why she looked familiar, she'd have been to the church with flowers – he didn't need any complications in his life. Anyway she was probably happily married – everybody was – and he most certainly wasn't interested!

CHAPTER 2

Lavinia Davenport watched the vicar drive away in his old blue BMW. She hadn't recognized him until he'd turned round and she'd seen the dog collar but then she'd never had occasion to speak to him before. The only time she set foot in his or any church was to dress it with flowers for a wedding but even then not always, often the church committee members liked to do their own arranging where possible unless bridal parties requested otherwise. One of her drivers would deliver the flowers and often any dealings she'd had with the church had been with the verger. If she had spoken to Steve it would have only been hello in passing.

He seemed a nice sort of a guy but it was unlikely their paths would cross again. She was no churchgoer, at least not since childhood. Her memories of such establishments were of her wedding to the lying cheating weasel Jez who'd wanted half of her business when she'd divorced him. As if! She'd worked too hard at it to give any of it to him and his latest floosie. She'd had a couple of relationships after him but had soon drawn the conclusion you were better off without a man. Oh they were all very charming at first, when they wanted you, but once the novelty began to wear off you took second, third, fourth, place to their mates, sport, the pub, other women – new challenges to display their charms to like the strutting peacocks they were. No, she'd had it with men. Anyway what was she thinking? She'd never have designs on a vicar. Could you just imagine tea on the lawn with all the old dears? She didn't think so. Her thoughts turned to Bernard her deceased neighbour.

He and his wife Esme had been good to live next door to. They'd had a market stall, greengrocery, a profitable business. Both had lost their parents within a short space of time of each other and were in their forties around the millennium when these houses were built so had invested monies from their inheritance into this property. She herself hadn't moved in until later. It was her little indulgence and one in the eye for Jez. He could keep his succession of women, she was happier with her home – *hers*, just how she liked it! It peed him right off to see her doing so well. It was a bit of a stretch for her financially and when Covid 19 had come along it had been a mixed blessing. She never wished ill on people but funerals were a large part of her business and during the pandemic numbers soared. She'd also qualified for the government's grant for businesses so it had been win win for her. The loss had come from weddings. Many were cancelled so she'd taken a hit there but she'd made a profit – just – and managed to stay afloat until life had returned to normal.

She'd make a special wreath for Bernard. She'd always been fond of him. He'd often given her cuttings and seedlings from his plants for her own garden, thus, many of hers were his babies. There was a beautiful white hellebore that he had the momma to, that always put on a good show in January, braving the snow and frost. Her hydrangea was one of his babies although he always coloured his to keep it blue where she let it do its own thing and flower pink for the acidity of the soil. He would always give her a tomato plant but hers never did as well as his. This year's would be more poignant as he wouldn't be around to nurture his to fruit and they'd wither and die on the vine.

Then there was his cat, Koko, a beautiful seal point Siamese. He and Esme had got her from a kitten but she was old now, must be fourteen or fifteen Lavinia reckoned. She'd liked to have taken her in, kept her on familiar territory but she was allergic to her. Regular cats just made her sneeze but the fine fur of a Siamese made her wheeze until she couldn't breathe, but luckily Frank's son had given her a home in her old age. Lavinia wondered how she'd adapt, if she'd miss Bernard and her life and whether she'd pine and die but at least she'd have a comfortable home and be taken care of. She set off back to work, she'd only called in back at home on a late morning break to check on the post.

The scent of flowers greeted her as she entered the shop, her favourite scent in all the world; she wished she could bottle it. The buckets of flowers on the floor, the vases on the display units around the walls, racks of cards to accompany bouquets along with decorations of butterflies, bees, teddies etc all in various colours to compliment the flowers, her domain. She had a good team of staff around her, sales staff with their own creative skills, delivery drivers, and she liked everyone to be able to cover each other in cases of emergency, staff absences with family illnesses etc, all had children except her – she had nephews and nieces – so time off was often needed at short notice and the business still had to run.

"All OK Jen?" she asked her right hand woman as she returned.

"Yes, no problems, well nothing that wasn't sorted. Carl had a puncture on the delivery van but he changed the wheel and carried on. Just need to get a new tyre."

"OK I'll see to that today."

The bell pinged and a regular customer walked in.

"Afternoon ladies. Beautiful day," Charles Lewis said as he searched among the buckets of flowers.

"Certainly is," replied Lavinia, "June has been lovely so far hasn't it. More flowers for Celia?"

Charles nodded with a bashful smile beneath his neat grey beard as he selected a bunch of fragrant white and pink lilies. "Lilies for my love."

"She's a lucky lady."

"Oh I'm the lucky one."

Most people in the village knew of Charles' next door romance with author Celia Wainwright. They'd got together in 2019 just before the Covid 19 pandemic and had a very satisfactory relationship living alongside each other, having their own space but just enough company. It seemed to work for them. The tea shop in the village, The Singing Kettle, was their favourite hangout and they could often be found there taking afternoon tea. Charles bought Celia flowers every week and extra on special occasions such as Valentine's Day, birthdays, anniversaries and such. Now there was a man who defied Lavinia's jaded view. Pity there weren't more like him around!

CHAPTER 3

Noel Williamson felt he'd come a long way since he'd been confused and alone in St Luke's church and he'd always be grateful to the police officer Jack Adams and the vicar Steve Oswald. In his mind they'd saved him.

He'd entered the church carrying a knife, under God's instruction. His mother had been killed in a hit and run accident and God kept telling him he had to avenge her death. He was her son and if he didn't do it who would? He should go to the church for divine guidance on who should die.

The divine guidance had come in the form of Jack and Steve who'd arranged counselling with Brian Welsh. All had rescued him and he was over that hurdle now. Jack had told him that the drink driver had been brought to justice so that chapter could be laid to rest. Brian Welsh had helped him come to terms with the burning anger, to understand that it was all part of the grieving process. He need never feel alone again, he would always have the three of them if ever he had any problems.

He did feel alone though. There had only been him and his mother and now she was gone. He was twenty and alone. He'd never had friends, no-one had accepted him, never had girlfriends, he felt they laughed at him, called him weird. He hadn't fitted in with anyone. He didn't have pets, didn't feel he could care for a living creature. He fed the birds in the garden and tended the plants in the rented property he'd shared with his mother. Hers had been the only love he'd ever known and he missed her terribly.

Tears formed in his eyes whenever he thought of her. Her gentleness, her vulnerability, yet she'd had a hidden strength. They'd escaped an abusive relationship with his father. Memories of that man were vague and unpleasant, his mother's screams, his father's raised voice, loud bangs as items were thrown around or smashed. He never knew what his mother had done wrong but one day she'd picked him up early from nursery school. He'd been playing in the sand when the teacher had come to get him.

"Mummy's here Noel, let's go and get your coat."

His mother had several bags with her, all that she could carry of their belongings and his favourite toys.

"Good luck Maisie," the teacher had said giving her a hug, and she'd squeezed Noel's hand. "Bye Noel. Be a good boy for Mummy."

That had been the last he'd seen of their old life. The council had housed them away from his abusive father and they'd had a good life on their own.

His mother worked in the warehouse in Tesco, away from the shop floor where she would be seen, she needed to stay out of sight in case he came looking for her. They'd moved to a different town ten miles away but he could have found them if he'd tried. Thankfully he didn't and they were left in peace.

As Noel grew up he followed in his mother's footsteps and worked in Tesco's warehouse. It was a steady regular job and he was happy, kept himself to himself, didn't get involved with people, just passed day to day pleasantries.

There was one girl he liked though, Colette who worked on the tills – one of the few remaining tills that weren't self service! He didn't approve of self service checkouts, doing people out of jobs. What if it did Colette out of a job? He'd never see her again! It would be like his mother. Someone else gone from his life.

Colette didn't think he was weird, well he didn't think she did. She always had a kind word for him.

"Hey Noel, how are you doing?" Her cheerful pretty face and curly brown hair always got his day off to a good start if he passed her in a morning.

"Good Colette thanks, are you?"

"Yeah, I'm good too. Catch ya later."

He didn't dare hope she liked him, not in *that* way, girls didn't, but she'd accepted his friend request on Facebook.

He'd been so nervous about sending it. His heart had pounded, palms sweated, breath had come in short gasps but he'd done it. He'd had to refrain from looking if she'd accepted but he was delighted when she had. He'd stalked her on there for weeks. How did you define stalking? How did liking someone differ from unhealthy obsession? It wasn't unhealthy obsession was it?

She wasn't in a relationship. How would he feel if she was? Angry? Disappointed? Hurt? He couldn't feel hurt because he had no right to. She didn't belong to him. He knew she'd never be his, he was just happy to worship her from afar but he'd be devastated if she got a boyfriend. Yes, that was the word, devastated.

Did he think he'd ever have a girlfriend? He'd never even kissed a girl, well not properly anyway, only quick playground games, a peck on the cheek. Was he destined to live his life alone and how did he feel about that? He'd never analysed his life before the sudden death of his mother but now he found himself thinking about it more and more. As a person he was quite self contained, content with his own company, but was this it now? Was this to be his life?

CHAPTER 4

Theo Stanyer was a neighbour of Bernard Wilshaw, living across the road and a little further down. He didn't sleep well, suffering from long covid and often watched Bernard washing his hands for many minutes on nocturnal trips to the bathroom.

Theo lived with his partner of several years, Donna Watson. The house was hers but she'd asked him to move in before the Covid 19 pandemic had hit. He'd been perfectly healthy, a chauffeur with a thriving business, a widower with two adult children Ross and Saskia. Then he'd picked up Covid in March 2020.

He hadn't been too ill, no worse than a bad attack of flu, a few days in bed, no hospitalization, but the malaise had never left him and he had been unable to drive. It would have cost him his business and his livelihood if it hadn't been for a suggestion from

Jade, Donna's daughter, to drive one of his clients for him, and it had sown the seed to employ a driver – which had become two – and thus his business had recovered after Covid, which was more than could be said for Theo himself. Recently however he was noticing slight improvements in his well being after following the advice of a nutritional therapist that he'd found online. Baby steps but he was able to do a little more, manage his condition better, the pacing was more beneficial and his recovery time from post exertional malaise was shorter. Thus, he was taking a short lunchtime walk as he saw Lavinia Davenport, Bernard's neighbour getting out of her car as she sometimes called in at home for lunch.

They greeted each other with a friendly, 'Hi, are you OK?'

"Very sad news about your neighbour," Theo remarked, not wishing to appear nosy but wanting information just the same.

"Yes, Bernard was such a lovely man. I don't think he ever got over losing Esme, his wife but they'll be reunited in Heaven now."

"Yes, a lovely thought isn't it. I feel for him on that; I lost my wife when our children were young."

"Oh I'm so sorry. That couldn't have been easy for you."

"No it wasn't but they were good kids and never brought me any trouble. Both married with babies now, well my son Ross and his partner Josie have never felt the need to marry. Whether they will or not I don't know. As long as they're happy that's the main thing isn't it."

"It is. My marriage broke up. Infidelity on his part, so I'd be very reluctant to try again." She nodded towards Theo and Donna's home. "You two seem happy."

"We are. I was quite wary about moving in together, giving up my own home, I'd been single a long time – well, disastrous second marriage after Tish died but I won't go into that – but Donna came along and it just seemed right. I think you know when something feels right don't you."

Lavinia pulled a face. "I can't say I would, no. My experience with my ex has put me off men for life. I couldn't go through that again."

"We're not all bad," Theo reassured her with a smile. "Take your neighbour Bernard."

She looked fondly towards his house. "No I suppose not. He was such a good man."

"I used to see him washing his hands at the bathroom sink in the middle of the night." In explanation to her quizzical expression he added, "I don't sleep too well and often brew up in the small hours if I'm wide awake. He seemed to be at the sink for ages with the light on."

Lavinia laughed. "I think he had a touch of O.C.D. His house was immaculate, and his garden and greenhouse. Everything was filed and labelled. Considering he loved his garden you never saw him with dirty nails. Perhaps that's what he was doing, scrubbing his nails?"

"In the middle of the night?"

She shrugged. "Who knows? Anyway, must go, I'll have to get back to work shortly."

"Yes, see you."

Theo envied her getting back to work. He was only approaching fifty and should still be able to work. He missed driving for his job. It had taken him all over the country, he'd driven miles and thought nothing of it. Now he couldn't even drive to visit Ross and Saskia a mere ten miles away. Donna did the driving when they visited. She didn't mind, she enjoyed driving but he'd have loved to have done it or at least taken a turn. Now he only managed short drives locally on his better days and that was when the anxiety allowed as well as his physical restrictions. However the anxiety wasn't as violent under the nutritional therapist's diet plan so he was daring to hope it was abating. He'd never have believed that what you ate – or more specifically the chemicals in the food that you ate – could have such an effect on the body. He'd never been one for diets, other than to try and eat fairly healthily but never tailored it to any one thing. Now here was this amazing woman suggesting what he should eat to improve various systems in his body and he was feeling slightly less ill.

He was still a million miles from being well though. Another area he felt he missed out on were his grandchildren. Aged two years now they were growing fast, very active and exhausting even for healthy grandparents. Those restricted by any form of chronic illness didn't stand a chance of babysitting. They did together, he and Donna, but as with the driving she did the care of the children, the hands on business. He was only able to partake in a little light play activity.

However they were a delight: Saskia and Richie's daughter, Ivy Evelyn, born February 2021 and Ross and Josie's daughter Summer Lily born a month later in March. It was a joy to watch them together. Even from this young age it was clear they had formed a close bond and would be great friends as well as cousins.

He did count his blessings. He found that the attitude of gratitude had a positive effect on his mental health. It wasn't easy on worst days but on better days he found he could cope with his situation if he focussed on what he could do rather than what he couldn't. His children were settled and happy, he had two beautiful granddaughters and a loving partner in Donna. Life could be a whole lot worse.

CHAPTER 5

Steve was driving to meet Frank Wilshaw, brother of the deceased Bernard. As he passed the flower shop he saw the woman who owned it outside adjusting some flowers in buckets. What had she said her name was? Ah, Lavinia, that was it. He ran his finger under the dog collar, it was another warm day and he had the car windows down. Lavinia looked up as he drove past and raised her hand in a wave. He smiled and waved back. Nice woman.

He arrived at Frank's house at 10 a.m. as agreed and was welcomed inside. Frank was alone apart from his black Labrador; his wife was at work.

"Morning Vicar, come inside."

"Thanks, and call me Steve, much less formal."

"Would you like a coffee?"

"I'll have tea please if it's no trouble."

"None at all. Have a seat in the lounge and I'll be through in a second."

He showed him into the bright east facing room of the smart detached house on the modern Beechwood estate and Steve looked at the family photos in frames around the room whilst he got out his diary. The dog made a great fuss of the newcomer with all his Labrador sturdiness, stuffing his nose under Steve's hand to get his ears scratched.

"What's your name then eh?" Steve asked rhetorically and the dog mumbled a slobbery reply, tail wagging wildly.

"Roman," supplied Frank returning with their drinks and biscuits, "and he'll have all that fuss all day long."

"He's a lovely boy aren't you." Steve gave the silky ears an exuberant rub and the dog was ecstatic.

"It wasn't suicide you know," Frank stated taking a seat in the armchair. "Had you been told?"

"I haven't been updated on that yet, no. What was the verdict?"

"It was inconclusive, accidental death. He'd fallen down the stairs and his neck was broken." His voice cracked with emotion. "Nobody can say if he did it on purpose or if he tripped and fell. There was no suicide note, only a few sheets of paper with his wishes among his documents." Frank leaned forward in his chair with a conspiratorial whisper, "Or was he pushed by the spiritual hands of Esme, his wife? I can say this to you Vicar, you being a man of the cloth and being spiritual. My wife thinks I'm raving mad to think that but it's possible isn't it. She was very possessive Esme, didn't like him spending time with anyone else, she probably wanted him with her. What do you think Vicar – sorry, Steve?"

Steve was very matter of fact. Grief affected people in many different ways and he always listened and tried to understand their thinking, trying to offer a suitable and comforting explanation.

"Well nothing is impossible is it but I wouldn't have thought a loving wife would have wanted to end her husband's life prematurely."

"She'd convince herself he couldn't be happy without her and want to take him to her."

"It was quite some years ago that she died though wasn't it."

"Aye it was but you can never tell can you."

"Was he unhappy do you think?"

"He was a bit melancholy at times but he loved the garden and he loved their cat Koko. He wouldn't have wanted to die and leave her with no-one to look after her."

"How's she doing? I believe your son took her in?"

"Yes he did. She's comfortable but she misses home, just lies in her bed in the conservatory. They bought all her familiar items with her: several beds, cushions, toys etc so it was a bit homely for her. When she does come out of her bed she miaows a lot as though asking for Bernard. She's an old girl and you can't explain to animals can you."

"No it's always very sad for them." Steve took a sip of his tea. "Shall we get on to the service? Have you discussed with the family what hymns and music you'd like?"

"We have yes. Hymns, we'd like All Things Bright and Beautiful because he loved his garden, and Jerusalem for England's green and pleasant land. For music he liked Enya. Leave the church to Only Time."

"Yes, good choices. Are you having flowers or donations?"

"Flowers because he loved them. We've ordered a family wreath from Say it with Flowers, you know, the florist on the main road."

"Yes I know." Funny how it/she kept coming into his head of late. Coincidence. Bound to happen. He must have had hundreds of dealings with the florist in the past for weddings, funerals, carnivals etc but never paid it any attention until they'd actually spoken the other day. That's all it was, putting a face to a name, or the business name. "Any special prayers?" He asked Frank.

"We'll leave that to you, not very well up in prayers."

"What about the eulogy? Is there a family member who wants to read it or do you want me to?"

"Oh you please. None of us are up to public speaking."

"Have you got some notes then of anything in particular you want to say?"

"I can't remember a lot of dates."

"It doesn't need to be detailed, you can just keep it to special family memories if you like or perhaps accolades or awards he had from work, hobbies, that kind of thing."

"I've just jotted these down." Frank got up and went over to a cabinet and took out a sheet of paper that he'd written ideas on and handed it to Steve who had a quick look through.

"That looks fine. If there's anything else you can think that you'd like to add you can always ring me or email. Have you sorted out a date with the funeral directors yet?"

"Not yet but I'll let you know as soon as they get back to me and see how it fits with you."

"OK great." Steve rose to his feet and Roman came up for another ear scratching. "I'll be off then. Thanks for the tea and biscuits."

CHAPTER 6

Steve's next officiation was an altogether more uplifting one, the baptism of Jake and Helena Hetherington's second child, a daughter, Daisy Jane, born the previous August 5th, making her almost eleven months old, sister to Noah Jacob, now two and a half. He'd known the family with its trials and tribulations from way back in the early days of his career when he'd first taken over as vicar of the parish. Chloe O'Keefe had then been married to Adam Hetherington, Jake had been a baby and a terrible car accident had resulted in Adam losing a leg. Chloe had met Nathaniel O'Keefe, a second child, Josh had come along to her and Adam, they'd tried hard to make their marriage work but it had ended in divorce. Both had subsequently remarried and each had a daughter with their new spouse. Steve knew them all well and it was always a joy to be a part of their family occasions.

It was the Saturday evening, the night before the service, and he was going over the last minute preparations in the church with Sue Thomas the verger when Noel Williamson walked in. Steve's heart sank just a little and he immediately reprimanded himself for the uncharitable feeling because he saw Noel as a soul in distress, but he was tired after a long day at a charity event for the Douglas MacMillan Hospice and he just wanted to get home for a light supper and a beer in front of the TV, and Noel could be a long job.

Sue made a discreet exit to put the baptism service booklets out for the next day and left Steve to it. He put on what he hoped was a welcoming smile.

"Noel. What can I do for you?"

"Hi Steve. I'm not disturbing you am I?"

"No," he lied, knowing he wouldn't be cursed to damnation because it was a white lie. "Just finishing up here then I'm done for the day." Oops, was that a mistake? Did it sound as though he had all the time in the world? He hoped not. His stomach rumbled to remind him not to let it drag on too long. "Is something worrying you?"

"Um…" Noel shuffled his feet and twisted his hands, blushing a little. "Well it's er… there's a girl I like at work."

"Ah. Affairs of the heart. I don't know if I'm the best one to advise you there. Not been very successful myself."

"It wasn't really that, it's more what I've done."

Ye Gods he wasn't going to say he'd raped her was he! How on earth would he offer advice on that? "And what *have* you done?" he asked a lot more calmly than his racing brain would have suggested.

"I've stalked her on Facebook."

Steve almost laughed out loud with relief after the horror stories he'd had mental images of. "Is that all? I thought you were going to tell me something drastic."

"Isn't it sinful to stalk people?"

"Well it is of course if it becomes an obsession and a danger to the person concerned but I hardly think looking someone up on Facebook is a sin, everybody does it."

"But I've found out she's got a sister who's just had a baby and I've seen all the photographs, and of her parents and the dog and everything."

"If that's all you've done Noel you've got nothing to worry about. We all look people up then you might have a mutual friend who you end up looking up and before you know it you're on holiday with them. Now if you'd said you'd followed her home I'd be a bit more concerned. You haven't have you?"

Noel was aghast. "Oh no Vicar! I'd never do anything like that. I don't even know where she lives."

"Have you asked her out?"

"Good grief NO! I'd never dare."

"Why not?"

"She'd never fancy me."

"How do you know?"

"I just don't get that vibe from her."

"How long have you known her?"

"Not long. I can't remember when she came to work here, I just gradually noticed her. She was always pleasant and friendly but that's all. We don't get into any kind of big chats, haven't been on the same lunchbreaks or anything. We only exchange pleasantries."

"Oh well just take it a day at a time and see how it all pans out."

"So the Facebook thing is OK then?"

"Perfectly fine. If she's accepted you as a friend allowing you to see her personal photographs she'll expect that you'll see her family. Just don't get too heavy eh."

Noel relaxed visibly, the cloud that had hovered over him threatening rain evaporating to sunshine. "Thanks, I won't. I'll be off for my tea now and I'll bet you're ready for yours."

"Certainly am. Take care, Noel."

CHAPTER 7

It was a fine July Sunday morning for the baptism of Daisy Jane Hetherington. Not too hot; not too cold. The blessing was a brief respite in the torrential downpours since the June heatwave had broken and although the skies were blemished with scudding grey clouds, they magnanimously held onto their moisture with good grace and allowed glimpses of sunshine, hot at this time of year, which took the edge off the peevish breeze billowing the ladies floaty dresses.

Inside the church the scent of lilies, arranged by Say it with Flowers, hung heavy on the air. Behind the altar with its embossed gold cloth and tall white candles flanking the gold cross in the centre, valiant sunbeams streamed through the vibrant reds, greens, blues and yellows of the stained glass windows and dust motes danced in their rays. The Reverend Steven Oswald stood before the congregation, resplendent in emerald green robe to welcome them all to worship. The baptism of Daisy Jane would be a part of the Eucharist service. After the initial section he invited parents and godparents to bring the child to be baptised to the font. Godparents chosen were Josh and Jade, Jake's brother and his partner, Liliana his half sister and Erica, Helena's sister.

The service progressed during which The Reverend addressed congregation, parents and godparents in turn.

'Will you support this child as she begins her journey of faith?'

'We will.'

'Will you help her to live and grow within God's family?'

'We will.'

To the parents and godparents with The Decision he asked,

'Do you reject evil?'

'I do.'

'Do you turn to Christ as Saviour?'

'I do.'

He signed the child with the sign of the cross. She looked quizzically at him as if to say, 'What's going on?'

After the Prayer over Water came the Profession of Faith and he asked,

'Do you believe and trust in God the Father?'

The congregation responded,

'I believe and trust in Him.'

Water was poured over the child and The Reverend said,

'Daisy Jane I baptise you
In the name of the Father
And of the Son
And of the Holy Spirit.'

The congregation responded,

'Amen.'

A lighted candle was presented to the newly baptised child, which she immediately reached towards and had to be held back! The Reverend then said a prayer of welcome followed by The Lord's Prayer and invited the congregation to share in the greeting of peace. This section always amused Steve because non church goers usually felt quite uncomfortable trotting round each other muttering, 'Peace be with you,' and many variations of, 'Oh, hello,' 'How do,' 'Hiya,' 'How are you?' and any other greeting people could think of were shared.

The service drew to a close with The Reverend saying,

'Go in peace to love and serve the Lord.'

The response.

'In the name of Christ, Amen.'

Everyone began to file out of the church and Reverend Oswald bid them all a jovial farewell, as was his manner. A warm and caring man, much loved by his parishioners he had a kind word and a smile for everyone and his resonant laugh rang out at any gathering.

"You're coming over to the village hall aren't you Steve?" Adam Hetherington, Jake's father, the baby's grandfather asked him. A tall, good looking accountant, always immaculately dressed, corn coloured hair now showing a sprinkling of grey making him look more dashing than ever, Adam had worn a prosthesis for many years, since the car accident when Jake had been a baby which had cost him his leg but no-one would have known. He'd had a below knee amputation and now only bore the slightest trace of a limp. He'd worked hard on his rehabilitation, determined to get his life back, and he'd succeeded. His first marriage to Chloe, Jake's mother might have failed but his second to Caitlin was a success, with daughter Ella now seventeen and growing into an attractive young woman. She was at college taking A Levels, one of which was English literature, her first love and she worked weekends in a small bookshop called PageTurners in the neighbouring village of Lower Hayfields. He was stepfather to Saba, Caitlin's daughter from a previous relationship, who was Jake's age but who had never had time for Adam's family and today was no exception. She was now grown and flown and busy with her own life.

"You bet!" replied Steve. "Can't wait for a slice of that cake I saw going in there earlier."

"Excellent! Me neither. See you in a bit."

Guests filed into the village hall to greet the newly baptised infant, looking adorable in her frothy white lace christening dress with matching headband on her dusting of fair curls. Her brother Noah was more interested in the pink and white balloons and wanted to know when he could have a piece of the christening cake.

"Later darling," soothed his mother, looking every bit as attractive as her daughter but wearing a pink and white sheath dress to match the cake, Jake in matching pink tie and pale grey suit which set off his blond colouring.

Godparents Josh and Jade walked up to take photos of parents and baby.

"Your turn next," said Jake handing the baby to Jade for more photographs. "Are you looking forward to it?"

Jade lovingly placed her free hand on her just visible bump. "We are aren't we Josh but nervous at the same time."

"Yeah, it's quite daunting to think that this time next year we'll be parents," Josh concurred.

"I know," grinned Jake, "I can't believe my baby brother is going to be a dad."

Liliana joined them with boyfriend Ryan. "Can I have a hold please? Are you coming to your Auntie Lili Daisy?"

Liliana hadn't inherited the blonde hair and fair complexion of Chloe their mother but the dark Romany looks of Nathaniel O'Keefe, her father and Daisy was fascinated by the lustrous tumbling dark curls. Indeed all the young women had long hair, her mother's and Jade's also dark but a different texture to Liliana's and Daisy was just at that age where it was intriguing to her to grab handfuls of this tactile stuff. She appeared to be quite happy being the parcel in this party game of pass the parcel among her aunts and uncles. Grandparents whilst just as eager to join in the game let the young people have their turn first. Helena's parents Mark and Alexa Barber had the children one day a week since Helena's maternity leave had ended and she'd returned to work.

A local catering company had laid on a delicious buffet of a selection of sandwiches, sausage rolls, pizza bites, Scotch eggs, salad, with strawberry cheesecake and a chocolate gateau for dessert, and the cake had been created by Dreams in Sugar, another local business.

Much as Helena as mother of two young children had her hands full she couldn't help but notice that her sister Erica hadn't eaten much and was looking rather pale beneath her make up. As soon as she could get her alone she asked her about it.

"I'm pregnant," said Erica.

Helena was shocked into silence for a second. Erica had been going out with Harvey from the sports shop where she worked for a few months. She'd fancied him for ages and been ecstatic when he'd asked her out at last. Erica was a bit naïve and at age twenty the last of her friends to lose her virginity so Helena hoped she hadn't rushed into anything.

"How far?"

"Eight weeks."

"Have you told Mum and Dad?"

Erica shook her head.

"What about Harvey?"

She nodded.

"How does he feel?"

She shrugged. "He was a bit quiet, not exactly overjoyed but he said we'd be OK."

"Will he stick by you?"

Again Erica shrugged looking tearful this time. "I'm not sure of him. I really love him, you know how much."

Helena nodded. She hated to see her sister upset but she couldn't hug her for fear of drawing attention to them.

"I don't know if he's ready for commitment," Erica continued. "I think that's probably why he didn't come today. He could have booked it off work if he'd tried. I don't think he can face babies." Her purple tendrils quivered as she tried hard to hold onto her emotions.

"Let's go outside," suggested Helena, "and you can tell me more."

Erica's tears flowed then and Helena held her tight. "We're here for you if you need us, don't forget that. You'd better tell Mum and Dad; they will be too."

"I know."

"Have you discussed the future with Harvey?"

"I daren't really. I don't want to push him into anything."

"Would you want to move in together, be a family?"

"More than anything, if it's what he wanted, but he's gone very distant, doesn't seem to want to kiss me or hold my hand. He was talking to Gemma at work the other day. He seems to get on well with her – too well!"

"Is there anything between them?"

"I don't think so but that doesn't mean he doesn't want there to be. Oh Helena I don't want to lose him but I think I am – and how will I cope with a baby on my own?"

Helena held her tighter while she sobbed. "You've got your family, and anyway you don't know if Harvey's going to leave you yet. It could just be initial shock. Give him time to get used to the idea and it might not all be as bad as you think." She reached into the slim pocket of her dress and pulled out a tissue. "Here, go to the loos and have a tidy up. We'll sort it, don't worry."

CHAPTER 8

Another event in the church and Willows Dip calendar was the summer fete. An enjoyable event? Well that was debatable when you took into account the backbiting of the committee members during all the planning of it. Some of the older members were set in their ways and objected to change. Younger members consisted of parents from Cranberry primary school PTFA with whom they collaborated for the event with their pupils being rose queen and her retinue. There was always a parade around the village on floats with a fancy dress and as long as tradition was upheld the older generation were happy. Steve remembered shocked gasps at the introduction of a disco in his younger days but those members were long gone and the disco was a fixture to follow the crowning of the rose queen.

A new rector had recently been appointed, Reverend Keith Simpson, a dour man in his early sixties. Steve thought he was counting down to his retirement and he hoped he wasn't going to come in and start making changes. He supposed he himself in his mid fifties could be said to be a touch staid, he did like everything done his way, and by and large his team worked well together. He didn't want anyone coming in and rocking the boat. Keith with his balding hair and deadpan expression put him in mind of Lurch from the Addams Family. A man of few words, you felt his malodorous presence digesting all of your hard work and not finding it palatable. However, he hadn't voiced any obvious complaints, apart from a bit of nitpicking about a misplaced hymn book or kneeling pad and Steve thought if that was all he could find fault with then he himself could hold his tongue until the man had left. His visits weren't as regular as they might have been so he must have been happy with the way operations were conducted at St Luke's. Perhaps he lurched over to other churches in the parish with less efficient vicars more often. Life ticked on without upset.

The two committee members who manned – or womaned – or was one supposed to say non gender specific nowadays – the refreshments were two spinster sisters, Lydia and Sadie Simcock. Now there was a pair if ever there was one. No wonder they'd never found a man between them. Sadie, the younger one, now late fifties, had sampled several men in her youth, usually belonging to someone else. It seemed to hold an added attraction for her if they were someone else's boyfriend or husband. Perhaps it was a challenge to lure them away. Her sister, Lydia, now early sixties, criticised everything she did: what she wore, her friends, the men. Not the warmest of women she had no time for her sister's affairs of the heart and the two of them were often caught bickering. They'd lived all of their lives in the house they'd grown up in and inherited on their parents' deaths, Sadie downtrodden and man hungry, Lydia a domineering sourpuss. On the quiet they were a source of great amusement to Steve.

"I don't know what possessed you to buy that coat," Lydia had jibed at Sadie one Sunday morning from their regular seat in the front pew. "It does nothing for you. Shocking pink never was your colour."

Sadie had looked mutinous. "Barry Smith always liked me in shocking pink."

"Whose husband was that and how many moons ago?"

"You're just jealous because men have never found you attractive."

"I wouldn't choose someone else's!"

Steve had had to turn away to hide the smirk on his face. He never knew how they managed to live together.

The day of the fete was mercifully dry amid a spell of low pressure, for which everyone was thankful. There was nothing worse than the rose queen's carefully dressed tendrils dripping in a downpour and her retinue shivering along behind her.

Connie Watson from Little Acorn Bird Sanctuary had come along with some of her birds to give a flying display as she did every year. It was always a popular show for both local people and visitors to the village alike. People, especially children, loved to hold the birds on the glove and have them fly to them. The snowy owls were always popular with hawks and kestrels being favourites too. Held in one of the farmer's fields there were lots of stalls and a marquee for refreshments with Lydia and Sadie holding sway.

Nathaniel O'Keefe walked in from his stall next door selling his bespoke carved furniture. He'd gained many of his regular customers from village fetes and craft fayres.

"Morning ladies. I'll have two teas to take away please," he said, turning that smouldering Romany smile on them. Only a few years younger than Sadie she'd never succeeded in luring that one away from his wife Chloe but it didn't stop the sweet smile and the push in front of her sister to fulfil his order.

"Mind you don't spill it Sadie," Lydia added spitefully, showing her up in front of Nathaniel so that Sadie's hands shook a little as she handed him the cups. She pushed in front of Sadie to take his money so that there was no chance of their hands touching.

Nathaniel took the cups. "Thank you. Have a good day."

"You can take that soppy look off your face," snapped Lydia, "you've got no chance there."

"How do you know? He likes blondes. His wife's blonde and Lara his first wife was blonde."

"Yes but they're natural. Yours is dyed."

Outside the marquee the sun shone and all of Willows Dip and surrounding areas seemed to have come for a look at the fete and browse the stalls. Donna Watson and Theo Stanyer had come with their neighbours Tess Barker and Billy Marshall from just outside Willows Dip. They lived in Regent Grove where Lavinia Davenport lived so it was a short car journey for them. They'd had a go on the tombola and Donna had won a jar of home made raspberry jam with a pretty red and white gingham cloth cap on it. They'd each bought cakes and cookies from the cake stall.

"Let's go for a cuppa," Theo suggested. "I need a sit down." Suffering from long covid his energy levels didn't last long and he needed to rest. Tomorrow would be payback for a day out.

Billy Marshall by contrast had suffered no ill effects from Covid 19. His work as a gardener kept him outdoors. Whether that had lessened the effects of the virus who could say but he'd been rather blasé to it even seeing the effect it had had on Theo. Nevertheless they were two attractive men to wander into the tea marquee much to Sadie's delight.

Lavinia had a stall with her cut flowers and they were selling well she was pleased to note. By lunchtime most were gone. She'd only caught glimpses of the handsome vicar as he'd mingled with the crowds and they'd exchanged pleasantries but that was all. It was quite sufficient, just enough to brighten the day, nothing more. It was proving to be a profitable day for her though. A young couple, both with brown dreadlocks came to her stall looking at the flowers.

"What do you think of these Ria?" the man asked the woman in a strong Australian accent.

She shrugged. "Not fussed. I'm not much of a one for flowers, you know that."

"They'll be nice for a treat and they'll brighten the place up a bit don't you think?"

"Yeah OK then."

He selected a bunch of pink carnations and handed them to Lavinia. "G'day. We'll take these thanks."

She wrapped them and handed them over then watched them walk away. The man had seemed pleasant but the woman hadn't seemed very grateful. He'd looked at her as though he really cared for her. How lovely to have someone look at you like that. The woman should think herself very lucky. She sighed. Ah well, only in dreams did that kind of love come along didn't it.

CHAPTER 9

Steve was with Noel at the City Dog's Home. It had all come about with the death of a parishioner, Syd Carson, leaving his little dog Macy all alone in the world. His family couldn't have her, she wasn't good with children, quite a nervous dog, so she was at the shelter waiting to be rehomed. Steve had spoken to the staff and had arranged to take Noel along for a visit, Noel being a loner could be quite a suitable companion for the dog. He'd broached the subject when Noel had sought him out on one of his many visits to the church. Steve sensed that he was lonely and in need of company by the frequent visits and thought that he and the dog could be good for each other.

"Something to run by you Noel," he'd begun one evening as they were straightening hymn books.

"What's that Vicar?"

"How would you feel about taking care of a little dog?"

Noel had gasped. "What permanently?"

"Yes. Your friend and companion. There's just such a little lady in need."

Noel looked uncertain. "Ooh I don't know. I've never had a dog before. I wouldn't know how to look after it."

"The staff at the shelter would help you, tell you all you needed to know, be there if you needed any advice. I could take you to meet her first, perhaps take her for a short walk. See how you get on. Her owner has died so she's grieving just like you and in need of some love. She's used to a single man's company, a quiet house, no noise. What do you think?"

"What's her name?"

"Macy."

"Oh, that's almost like my mum. My mum was Maisie. Perhaps she's trying to come to me through the dog." He became thoughtful for a second. "What about when I have to work?"

"The staff know this and she's OK with her own company. She does like her walks though. Syd used to take her over the common."

"Oh I can do that! It will be good for us both. OK then I'll come and meet her."

Margaret Flynn the supervisor at the shelter took them through to where a small cream and white Jack Russell/Shih Tzu cross lay tucked in her bed, her head resting on a pink teddy.

"Some visitors for you Macy. Are you going to come and say hello?"

Macy raised her head, large soulful eyes sad and lonely and Noel felt an instant connection with a kindred spirit. Macy knew Steve from his visits to her home and seeing him out on her walks and got out of her bed, stretched and waved her feathery tail at him. He in turn fussed her and Noel knelt down and let her sniff his hand. To his delight she took a liking to him as he had to her and Margaret suggested they took her to the play area to throw the ball for her and see how she bonded with Noel.

It went like a dream. Considering he'd never had a dog before he seemed like a natural with her and was delighted when during the games she climbed onto his knee and licked his face. After a short while she was returned to her kennel and Noel had a brief interview to ascertain his suitability to care for her. Another date was arranged for him to come and take her for a walk with one of the staff and if that went well a date would be set for him to collect her.

He couldn't wait! He couldn't remember being so excited since being a small boy waiting for Christmas. At the shelter he'd been given several leaflets on how to care for her, what food and vaccinations she'd need, treats and toys, and he wanted to make sure he gave her a good life. Steve thought she was about eight years old so not a boisterous young puppy but not an old dog either and they could have some good walks together.

He was a frequent visitor to the pet's department at work – always going through Colette's till.

"I'm getting a dog!" he'd told her, full of enthusiasm.

"That's great Noel! When?"

"Couple of weeks."

"What breed?"

"Jack Russell/Shih Tzu cross. Macy her name is, almost like my mum."

"Sounds lovely. I bet she's very pretty. How old?"

"About eight years we think. She's a rescue dog, her owner has died."

"That's sad for her. She'll need loads of love."

"She certainly will and she'll get it. I love her already!"

"I can tell you do."

Another customer had appeared, unloading goods onto the belt and Noel had had to move on but he'd been cheered by his chat to Colette and his purchases for Macy. She'd got her own beds from home which would be familiar to her but he hadn't been able to resist buying her another, a sumptuous padded affair that he'd just put in the living room and let her decide if she thought it was comfortable. He couldn't wait to bring her home.

CHAPTER 10

Harvey stopped his car outside the two bedroomed semi detached house on the Beechwood estate that he and Erica had come to view. Erica sat beside him, a multitude of feelings flooding through her: hope, despair, a tremor of excitement at their first home but sadness that he wasn't more enthusiastic about it, and love, always love for him and their unborn child.

He'd attended the twelve week scan with her and suggested they look for a house to rent. He hadn't appeared overjoyed, just matter of fact, as if seeing the image on the screen had made it real. That image hadn't appeared to move him and his facial expression had been impassive as the sonographer had pointed out details to them. Erica's own wonder and joy had been somewhat dampened by Harvey's lack of response. She'd been surprised therefore by his suggestion of them looking for a house to rent as they'd walked back to his car.

He hadn't taken her hand but had held the car door open for her, always polite, always gentlemanly, it was one of the characteristics she loved about him, his kindness. That was still there, the kindness. It was the love that was missing, or was it only masked by the shock of the situation he found himself in now? That was what she dared to hope.

They got out of the car and walked up the short drive to the front door of the house. It had a small lawn to the side and a low fence to the front and separating it from the neighbouring property. Harvey rang the bell and an agent opened the door.

"Mr Davies and Miss Barber?" she enquired.

They affirmed.

"Come in and I'll show you around."

The small square hall led to a living room on the left and stairs facing. It was unfurnished and both families had said they'd help them out with basics to start them off: sofa and chairs, dining table and chairs. They'd take Erica's double bed and Harvey's single but the second bedroom would be the nursery so furniture would be purchased for that in due course.

The living room had a plain grey carpet which Erica thought she'd get a rug to cover as it had seen better days, that was after it had had a good clean! That led into a fitted kitchen diner with duck egg blue walls and pale grey cupboards – very tasteful Erica thought. She cast surreptitious glances at Harvey, trying to read his thoughts but he wore the same impassive expression he'd worn at the scan, as if it was all a fait accompli to him and he was trapped on a merry go round he'd never wanted to get on in the first place and now couldn't get off. She felt like the fairground ride operator spinning it ever faster until Harvey felt more and more nauseous and unhappy with the whole experience. She sighed and followed the estate agent out into the back garden, which was beautiful. Two levels, both lawn, bordered by flower beds with shrubs along the bottom end and a stone bird bath.

"The landlord stipulates that the garden be kept tidy. There's a lawnmower in the garage and fortnightly compost bin collections from April to October. Are you gardeners?"

"We both help a bit at home," Harvey said.

"Yes we can keep it tidy," Erica added.

"Come back inside and I'll show you upstairs."

It consisted of front and back bedroom, the front with fitted mirrored wardrobes, and a bathroom with a white suite and shower over the bath. It looked clean and well maintained. Again Erica felt happy with it and could see herself here with their baby. If only Harvey were happy she would have been thrilled but as before his expression gave nothing away and his blue eyes looked sad as opposed to joyful.

"What do you think?" asked the agent.

"I like it," Erica said. "What about you Harvey?"

He shrugged and nodded.

"Go and discuss it," suggested the agent, "but get back to us as soon as you can, there's been a lot of interest."

They both thanked her and headed back to the car.

"Let's go for a drink," said Harvey starting the ignition.

They drove to a quiet pub away from the village and after getting their drinks from the bar, took them outside to a secluded corner table where they had some privacy.

"What did you think?" Erica ventured taking a sip of her coke. "Did you like it?"

He took a long drink of his lager, placed the glass on the table, his hands round it and looked down into it, blond hair falling over his eyes. He looked very young and innocent.

"It's a nice house. It just seems such a big step and I don't know if I'm ready for it; don't know if I'm ready to be a father, or for the commitment."

Erica's heart was pounding, not knowing what was coming next. "I'm sorry if I've trapped you."

"You haven't. We were both in it together, but it's all just taken a step we hadn't bargained for."

She took a deep breath. "You... you don't... want me to do anything about it do you?"

His head snapped up. "Termination? Good God no! I'd never think of that!" He ran his hand through his hair in an act of despair. "It's all such a shock. We'd never talked about the future and now here we are with it being forced in our faces. How do you feel?"

It was the first time he'd ever asked how she felt and she hoped it might be the first droplet of water in the thaw. "I could never consider termination and I'm glad you couldn't either. Whatever happens this is our child and is meant to be. So do we take the house? Is it what you want?"

"I don't know that it's what I want but I think it's what we should do if you agree."

"Yes I do."

"OK then I'll ring the agent when I get home."

They finished their drinks and walked back to the car. Still he didn't take her hand. There was just one question she couldn't help but ask.

"Harvey?"

"Yes?"

"Have you stopped loving me?"

She felt the shutters that had opened ever so slightly slam shut again with her words and she wished she hadn't asked but she had to know where she stood.

"I don't know."

CHAPTER 11

Steve had called into the post office/newsagent/general store in the centre of Willows Dip, directly opposite St Luke's church to get a sandwich for his lunch. They did delicious filled baguettes and he was particularly partial to tuna and cucumber on oatmeal bread. The store had recently been taken over by a young Asian couple, Jafar and Maryam Khan after the previous owners had retired, very pleasant, always had a smile for their customers and had settled into the village well.

That morning he had taken Noel to The City Dog's Home to collect Macy. Noel had been so excited and Macy had greeted them with equal pleasure as if she sensed the new adventure she was about to embark on. He had dropped them off at Noel's home and left the pair to get properly acquainted.

As he came out of the store he almost collided with Lavinia from the flower shop, and there beyond them on the frontage of the shops was the village eccentric, known to all as Mad Maurice. He fancied himself as a preacher and could be found at various locations in the village spouting forth his own incantations from the Bible: at the common, the churchyard, the shops, usually clad in grey attire, jeans, T shirt, jacket depending on the weather, his wild grey hair billowing around his head like a dandelion clock in the breeze, dead grey fish eyes focussed on nothing in particular, probably some divine vision in his head.

"And the Lord sayeth repent of the sin of avarice or ye shall be cast into eternal damnation." His palms were outspread, raised to the Heavens.

This was why Steve and Lavinia had almost collided, both of their attention was on Maurice.

"Oops sorry. Oh hi," they said in unison."

"Looks like your nemesis is here." Lavinia nodded towards the soothsayer.

Steve grinned. "He's beaten me to it this morning."

She chuckled a response. "Does he bother you with his misguided preachings?"

"Not at all. That's all he is, misguided. If it keeps him happy let him carry on, he's harmless enough."

"Well to those who know him."

"There is that yes. Are you on your lunch break?"

"Yes are you?"

He raised the baguette. "Sort of. I just grab it when I can."

"I do too really. Sometimes call in at home as I did the other day when we spoke. Any news on Bernard's funeral yet?"

"I've been to see Frank and I'm waiting for him to get back to me with a date from the funeral directors. I'll let you know as soon as I hear."

"Thanks, I'd appreciate that. I'd like to do an appropriate wreath for him. Anyway I'll go and see what baguettes they've got. That one of yours looks quite tasty. Good to see you."

"You too."

He walked away with a spring in his step. She really did give him a little lift and he didn't know why. As they were both on a lunch break he could have asked her to The Singing Kettle for a cup of tea, but then again no, that might start something and he didn't want to be starting anything with her or anyone, he'd had enough of that.

Lavinia too had felt a little heart skip. A pleasant interlude to popping out to get a bite to eat. He did seem a lovely guy but then she didn't want to go getting feelings for him or anybody. It only led to complications and ultimately heartbreak. She did wonder what he looked like in his full regalia though for his church services. Strangely she found that dog collar quite sexy. Steady on girl! Don't even go there! Perhaps it wouldn't hurt to go to a Sunday service though, see him in action so to speak, but then would he think she fancied him? That would never do would it. She'd ponder on it.

CHAPTER 12

The atmosphere was a little strained between Erica and Harvey and their families as moving day commenced. Both sets of parents were there, Mark and Alexa, Erica's parents, and John and Alison, Harvey's parents. Each went about any duties assigned by the young reluctant couple: cupboards and windows were cleaned, floors hoovered and mopped, beds assembled and made up with polite smiles and pleasantries exchanged.

Alexa and Alison did have a moment whilst making morning coffee for everyone.

"What do you make of all this?" broached Alexa.

Alison sighed. "They're not getting off to the best of starts are they. I think it's all come as a shock to them. Harvey has become really withdrawn whereas all he could talk about before was Erica. How's she taking it?"

"She's upset, thinks he doesn't love her. Physically she's fine. There's been a touch of morning sickness, we don't often escape that do we but all was well at the scan as you probably know."

"No not really. Harvey said nothing other than it was OK. He looked like a rabbit caught in headlights when he got home. We haven't seen a picture of the scan or anything."

"Give me your number and I'll send it to you. It's not fair you should be kept out of the loop. We're all grandparents."

She showed Alison the photo and they exchanged numbers before carrying the drinks through to the living room where everyone was having a rest. Alison was quite tearful at the image but regained her control before leaving the kitchen.

Erica, into her second trimester was looking well, her bump just beginning to show and under different circumstances this would have been a joyous occasion. The dads were talking cars, Mark was a mechanic and had a successful business in Hartford, the closest town to Willows Dip. Many of the locals took their cars to him for services and repairs. Harvey was as Alison had said, withdrawn.

As a mother Alison was worried about her son. He looked so young and vulnerable. He'd been so in love with Erica and she'd hoped he'd found 'the one.' Both she and John liked her and were happy for her to be the girl for their only son. Harvey had always talked to her about anything and they'd had a close mother son bond but he'd clammed up over this. A concrete fortress had been erected around him that no-one seemed to be able to penetrate. His father had made tentative steps to talk to him but to no avail. She wondered what was going on in his head. Was it a form of anxiety? You heard such terrible stories of suicide rates in young men. There always seemed to be vulnerable people jumping from bridges and she feared for her son and didn't know what to do to help him. If she tried to talk to him and chose the wrong words would it tip him over the edge? She didn't know what to do. With a worried look she handed him his mug.

"Tea son."

He gave her a wan smile. "Thanks Mum."

She so wanted to hold him in her arms, make it all go away, make it right for him. A little spark inside her was looking forward to her first grandchild, especially having seen the scan now, but how much more did she wish her son was looking forward to its birth too?

Later when everyone had gone, Harvey had wired the TV up, plus their own in their rooms upstairs, for the time being at least they were sleeping separately. It wasn't what Erica wanted but it was what she expected. At least he was in the same house as her. Maybe the closeness they'd had would return over time. This was the hope she clung on to, like the last desperate thread before a rope snapped, praying for a repair. They'd ordered a takeaway and she was putting it out onto plates in the kitchen to take and watch in front of the TV to relax.

"What do you want to watch?" he asked her coming through to help her bring the food and drinks in.

"I don't mind. What had you thought?"

"How about John Wick?"

"OK, sounds cool."

He sat in the armchair balancing his meal in one hand and the TV remote in the other and selected it; she sat on the sofa. They ate in silence, absorbed in the food and TV. When the film ended she cleared the plates away to wash up.

"I'll go for a bath after then go to bed, I'm tired after today. What about you?"

"I'll go on a game for a bit then check we've locked up and come up later."

"OK, goodnight then."

"Goodnight."

He managed a brief smile in her direction but that was all. She didn't know whether to feel pleased or sad. It was a trace of warmth but a far cry from the hot passion that had conceived their child, the glow of love they'd had for each other, but perhaps it was a start.

CHAPTER 13

Noel was walking Macy over the common between July showers, her nose investigating the scents that were familiar to her, feathery tail waving revealing her delight at being back roaming her territory. He hadn't quite dared let her off the lead as he wasn't confident enough in her coming back but it was extended to allow her a sense of freedom. Suddenly she stopped on spying a pure white cat coming towards them miaowing enthusiastically. In turn she began to bark, her tail waving wildly. Noel was uncertain what to do. Dogs and cats didn't like each other but these two seemed to contradict that. The cat ran up to Macy and began to rub its silken body around her and the dog was ecstatic. She whined joyfully in greeting and the cat's rumbling purr matched it.

"Well I never!" exclaimed Noel. "I wouldn't have believed it if I hadn't seen it with my own eyes."

A voice from behind him answered his vocal thoughts and he turned to see a young teenage girl with light brown dreadlocks and wearing a Beechwood High School uniform. "They're mates. It's Macy isn't it," she stated with an Australian accent.

"Yes it is," he replied. "How do you know?"

"That's Snowball my cat and they often meet up on their walks." She bent to scratch the cat's ears and he turned his head into her caress. "Well Snowball, and here I was thinking you'd come to meet me and all the time it's Macy you're pleased to see." She turned to Noel. "We used to see Syd walking her but I haven't seen them for ages. He's OK isn't he?"

Noel looked worried. "I'm sorry to be the bearer of bad news but I'm afraid he's passed away, which is how come I've got Macy."

Tears came into the girl's eyes. "Oh no! I'm so sorry to hear that. He was such a lovely man. We used to have bonza chats and he was very helpful to me for my history work, with his life experience and stories. How did he die do you know?"

"I'm sorry I don't, I only know about him from Steve – the Reverend Oswald when he suggested I might be able to look after Macy. She was at the City Dog's Home and looking to be rehomed. I'm Noel by the way."

"I'm Alicia Rose, just Alicia. Well I'm glad she's found someone to take care of her and she can keep her friendship with Snowball if you often walk this way."

"I do, but I will regularly now I know she has a friend here."

"That's good. Must be off. Catch you later."

He watched the girl walk away and the cat said his farewells to Macy and trotted after her. Noel wondered where they lived. There weren't many homesteads hereabouts. The girl – Alicia she'd said her name was – must be about thirteen or fourteen and Australian? How come she was living here? Perhaps he'd catch up with them again as she'd said she'd seen a lot of Syd. She seemed very friendly and he'd never had friends before. Maybe she'd be one?

CHAPTER 14

Welcome family and friends of our neighbour and loved one Bernard as we pass him into God's care."

The words of Reverend Steven Oswald rang out in St Luke's church to open the funeral service of Bernard Wilshaw. Many had come to pay their respects and say their goodbyes and it was clear that he'd been well thought of in the area. To his adoring congregation Steve looked seraphic in his funeral attire, white vestment over black cassock, the purple stole embellished with gold crosses giving him an evermore godlike quality. Godlike in an approachable way, not a distant, heraldic untouchable figure, he was always available for anyone who needed him and led his flock in a loving, brotherly rather than fatherly manner. Thus he led this service, giving off the warmth of his personality.

The warmth of his personality and the splendour of his appearance in his official capacity weren't lost on Lavinia Davenport,

Bernard's next door neighbour. When his resonant baritone spoke the words, 'I am the resurrection and the life,' it sent tingles down her spine. She was getting the hots for this kind, gentle but charismatic man and she absolutely could not let that happen. In the words of The Iron Lady, 'No. No. No.' Perhaps it was the will of The Lord and He was drawing her to him? What power would she have to resist then if it were her will against God's? But then if it was God's will could it be that it would be right this time? Could he be 'The One?'

'Don't be ridiculous woman!' snapped the voice of reason. 'The man's a vicar for Heaven's sake! You don't go around fancying vicars. Get real!'

She dragged her errant rambling thoughts back to the service and tried to concentrate them on the actual words rather than her burgeoning desires for the man delivering them. At that moment he looked her way and their eyes locked for several seconds. Time seemed to stand still. Her mouth went dry. How he continued to speak she didn't know, nor did she know what he was saying, she was only aware of that shared look between them. Her face felt flushed at the power of those few seconds but then it was gone and Steve began the eulogy.

He told of Bernard's childhood growing up with his brother Frank, of his Saturday job on the greengrocer's stall in the market, which had sparked his interest to get his own stall that had provided him with a livelihood. He'd met and married Esme through work and they'd enjoyed life having travelled the world on many foreign holidays.

As he spoke Steve got the scent from the lilies in the family wreath on the coffin and his thoughts were drawn to Lavinia who'd arranged them, as they had been a few moments before with that fleeting but powerful glance. Had she felt its power? Surely she must have done, it was too strong for her not to. Was God toying with them here in His house? He didn't have time to ponder on it, he had a service to conduct.

The service drew to a close with Enya's 'Only Time,' played on leaving the church as Frank had requested, and the mourners followed the coffin to the grave where Bernard would be laid to rest beneath the trees near the back wall with his dear wife Esme. Steve said a prayer and a blessing and thanked God for the life and love of Bernard.

Lavinia had felt a need to position herself close to Steve. It wasn't a conscious thought or a plan, it just kind of had to be; a sort of compulsion, a need to be close to him. There was no explanation to it, no thought, just something that drew her, as though his soul drew hers – but maybe that was a little fanciful. She'd already told herself NO, but something within her seemed to be taking control, not entirely against her wishes but against her better judgement. As they moved away from the grave she wondered whether she ought to speak to him or perhaps not as he was still 'on duty' as it were.

He spoke to Frank as they walked away and all had been invited to the village hall to the wake to remember Bernard. Her heartrate quickened as she thought they might get a chance to speak later. She moved across to have a look at the flowers.

Her own wreath she was pleased with. She'd chosen 'Blessings,' a coral coloured rose with a delightful fragrance, interspersed with gypsophila, baby's breath. Bernard had always loved roses and had Blessings in his garden so she knew he'd appreciate it if he was looking on in spirit. The family wreath she'd also done. White lilies, traditional for a funeral but always beautiful and fragrant. Others had come from other florists and she cast a critical eye over them, what she would have done differently, a tweak here, a twist there.

"Do they all meet with approval?"

Her heart recognized the resonant tones a split second before her brain did with her newly heightened senses and she turned to see Steve beside her, divested of vestments and now in black trousers and shirt with the dog collar that she was coming to find so sexy. "STOP!" screamed something somewhere as an image of Satan tempting Christ loomed before her. 'Don't get carnal desires about the vicar!'

She felt sure she'd blushed to the roots of her hair. "I was just casting a critical eye yes. Naughty of me isn't it but I can't help it, occupational hazard."

He laughed. "I suppose it is. Are you going over to the village hall?"

"Yes are you?"

"Yes. We'll walk together."

Her mouth had gone dry again so she said what everyone said but she did mean it. "Lovely service."

He looked pleased. "Did you think so?"

"I did. Very moving with the music and I always love the eulogy, hearing what the deceased had done throughout their life." She didn't add that he'd also moved her. Best keep that little snippet of knowledge to herself.

"I always like that too. It's especially poignant when there's been a lot of suffering towards the end of life, to imagine that person in their youth, young and vibrant, full of life."

"Tragic isn't it, the tricks life plays on us. We none of us know what it's got in store for us do we."

"No and probably just as well."

They'd reached the door of the village hall and Lavinia felt a little disappointed and slightly jealous that she'd have to let him go to others now, their brief time alone had come to an end.

"You said you enjoyed the service," he commented. "How about looking in on a Sunday Eucharist sometime?"

They turned towards each other and she nodded, a smile lighting up her face. "OK, I might just do that."

They walked in through the door and his adoring parishioners claimed his attention. Lavinia didn't get a chance to speak to him again but she spoke to Frank and mingled with other neighbours and friends. Before leaving she made a point of seeking Steve out. He was talking to two little old ladies holding tea cups and she got the tea-on-the-lawn image. She touched his arm lightly.

"Bye Steve, I'll see if I can get along to Sunday Eucharist."

He returned the touch to her elbow. "Bye Lavinia. It'll be great to see you if you can."

She stepped outside into the fine drizzle, typical of this July but her heart was singing. They'd touched! Physical contact! How had she dared! And he'd asked her to go to the Eucharist! Of course it wasn't a date and he would always want to add new members to his congregation but he wanted her presence there; she could only be pleased about that. She did have to shake a metaphoric finger at God though and she had a word of reprimand as she got in her car.

"What are you doing to me God? You're playing with me. Please don't cast me aside like a broken toy when you get tired of this game."

CHAPTER 15

Another pregnancy a little further along than Erica Barber was Jade Watson with fiancé Josh Hetherington-O'Keefe. Hers was quite a contrast to Erica's experience and she thanked Heaven for Josh's care and attentiveness. He couldn't have treated her better. She was a few years older than him, he early twenties, she late, and she always called herself his cougar, which he found amusing.

He often surprised her with flowers and took lots of photographs of her blossoming body. A professional photographer he wanted to capture each stage of her pregnancy from every angle, naked shots lying across the bed, draped in a chair, shots for their own private album, delighting in how her long, silky black hair fell over her full breasts as her pregnancy developed. She'd been reluctant at first in case anyone else should see the photos but as he had his own studio he assured her that no-one ever would. As she'd become accustomed to posing for him it had become quite erotic and had led to many loving and passionate moments between them and she had admitted to feeling sexy and sensual as she saw the desire etched on his face as his blond tousled locks fell over the camera as he concentrated on getting the best shot. There had been one image that he had managed to convince her to allow him to enlarge and put on canvas. It just showed her bump as she sat on a stool, long hair covering her breasts and a white chiffon wrap across her hips so that nothing personal was on display.

"Just for our bedroom," he'd pleaded.

"Oh go on then," she'd reluctantly agreed, secretly vowing to make sure nobody else ever set foot in there. As their child/children grew maybe the canvas would be hidden away, she'd decide later.

They didn't see Erica and Harvey other than in passing but heard of them through Jake and Helena, Erica's sister and Josh's half brother. It made her feel guilty how strained their relationship was and how unbearable it must be for Erica to feel unloved at just the time in her life when she needed the utmost love from her partner.

It was Jade's day off from work – she ran one of her mother Donna's boutiques, La Femme, in the nearby town of Wheaton-le-Moor – and she'd called into the post office store with a parcel to post. She'd said 'Hi' to Maryam but couldn't supress the smirk that came to her face when she saw who was on the post office counter. It was the forty something woman with the dark curly hair who attended the swingers parties in one of the houses on the new estate opposite hers and Josh's cottage; they'd spied on them several times! They never closed the curtains as if they got an extra kick out of onlookers seeing their liaisons and Jade and Josh never had need of porn movies with them across the road!

"Hi Sugar," she greeted Jade with a friendly smile, her name badge informing that she was Vicki, "just the parcel is it?"

"I need stamps and cash back please," Jade replied, unable to keep the images of the woman's more scantily clad form out of her mind. She was finding it difficult to look her in the face.

As Vicki prepared the parcel, sticking the first class postage on, Jade's eyes slid to her ample breasts in the too tight top and wondered how many different men's hands had been rummaging round them! STOP, she told herself, dragging her mind back to the job in hand.

"How much cash Sugar?" Vicki was asking.

"Sorry, I was miles away. Fifty pounds please."

"Put your card in."

Jade complied, wondering how many men she'd used that euphemism with. Vicki counted out the cash, gave out the stamps requested and bid Jade a cheery, "Bye Honey."

It was Jafar, manifesting from behind the herbs and spices who Jade greeted on her way out and she wondered just how much he and his wife knew of their staff member's social life. Good Muslim people would they approve of such behaviour? Well she wouldn't reveal Vicki's secret, she'd leave it up to her to do that.

Good grief, as she left the store there was Mad Maurice in his imaginary pulpit and she skirted swiftly round him and came upon Reverend Steve as she walked home along the lane.

"Hi Jade, are you keeping well?"

"Fine thanks Reverend Steve are you?"

"Can't complain. Plenty to keep me busy."

"I've just escaped Maurice and the swinger," she giggled, then realized perhaps she'd said too much to a man of God. "Oops sorry, just slipped out."

"Who's the swinger?"

There was no going back now so she told him all. "Vicki, the woman in the post office. You should see the sin and debauchery that goes on over the road from us. They need their immortal souls saving Vicar!"

Steve chuckled. "Word has reached me about some of the less savoury activities of the village but I'll perhaps leave that one to Maurice to sort out!"

Jade laughed. "I'm sure he could get his teeth into that den of iniquity. Oh, sorry, poor choice of words there."

They both laughed.

"Avarice seems to be his thing doesn't it," remarked Steve, "but then who knows, sin is sin. He might fancy a bit of variety." He patted her arm. "I'll be off now. I'm glad you're well. Take care."

CHAPTER 16

Noel was tending his mother's grave as he did frequently. He'd brought her carnations, some of her favourite flowers. Macy was by his side as she was whenever he wasn't working.

"I've brought your almost namesake along Mum. You'd have loved her if you'd met." He ruffled the dog's head and she wagged her tail in response. The two had become close companions.

He arranged the flowers in the pot after removing the dead ones. He got over most weeks but with work it wasn't always possible and he didn't like her grave to look neglected. He'd added small plaques with verses on to go with the headstone, which was quite basic as he wasn't financially able to run to anything fancy.

"I've had a disappointment in love Mum but I don't feel as bad as I thought I would about it, that's thanks to Macy here." He looked lovingly at the dog. "I think we were meant to be together.

I've liked Colette, a girl on the tills at work for quite a while but looking back she's only ever been friendly towards me. Well gossip around the store has it that she's started a relationship with a girl from the bakery. Lucy her name is, she has short green hair! I'd noticed they were friendly, sat together on lunch breaks, that kind of thing, but I didn't think in that way. There was never any chance for me was there if she prefers women to men! I'm OK about it though. I don't know if that's because it's a woman. Maybe I'd have been more jealous if it had been a man. Weird isn't it."

"You talk to them too," said a voice passing behind him as a blonde woman of about his age moved to a grave a bit further along.

He blushed feeling stupid. "My mum," he offered by way of an explanation.

"Ah, I'm sorry. Mine are my nan and granddad but I talk to them too, tell them about my life, trials and tribulations."

Noel relaxed and felt lighter although he hoped she hadn't heard what he'd been saying. "Glad it's not just me then."

"Nah, I think their spirits are always with us watching over us don't you?"

"I do. I feel my mum all the time."

"Is it long for you?"

"Last year. Road accident. What about you?"

"My nan eighteen months ago, cancer, my granddad soon after, broken heart, just wasted away. They were late eighties and had had a good life but it's never easy to say goodbye is it."

"No it isn't."

The young woman arranged her flowers as Noel had done for his mother, then stood back to look at them. "Roses," she said. "They both loved them but we have to buy what's in season don't we."

"Yes. My mum loved carnations. She liked lots of flowers really but carnations were her favourite. I've not seen you before. Do you often tend your grandparents' grave?"

"Fairly often. My mum comes as well, they were her parents. Are you a regular?"

"I try to be but can't always because of work."

"Where do you work?"

"Tesco. Warehouse."

"Oh, right."

"Where do you work?"

"Primark."

"Oh in town then."

"Yes so we're not far from each other."

"We might bump into each other on a lunch break. What's your name?"

"Krystina, what's yours?"

"Noel."

She wrapped her dead flowers up in the wrapping of the fresh ones, giving the fresh ones a tweak in the vase. "I'll look out for you then Noel when I'm on my lunch. Take care."

He watched her walk towards the bin to put the rubbish in and thought he should have asked for her number. He was always a bit slow on the uptake and thought after the event – should have done this, should have said that. With luck Fate would be on their side and he'd certainly have a look in the menswear department of Primark!

CHAPTER 17

Lavinia chose to sit at the back of the church for the Sunday Eucharist so as not to be obtrusive. As a child she'd attended Sunday school and even been confirmed along with her friends, she remembered wearing the white dress of satin and lace well, and the white patent shoes and ankle socks, but it had all dwindled when she'd hit her teens and nightlife had taken over. Now she had feelings of familiarity as she sat in the pew absorbing the ambience of the church. Perhaps it was stating the obvious to say that churches had a God like quality, or maybe that was what Christians were schooled to believe and so that's what they felt but whatever it was she always found it pleasant, calming and comforting and yes, now it was tinged with a sprinkle of excitement for the presence of its leader. They always had a distinctive smell too, churches. Not just the obvious candle wax but something she couldn't quite define. Again, as with the feeling, she just put it down as Godly, churchy.

She looked at the board at the front with the hymn numbers on and picked up the book in front of her to see what they were going to be singing. Something else she'd always enjoyed, singing hymns. A groan pulled at her soul when she saw the first one. Make Me a Channel of Your Peace. She hated it. Lots of people loved it, thought it was beautiful but to her it was just a boring dirge that droned on and on. She wouldn't enjoy singing that one. She flipped the pages to the next. Much better. Give Me Oil in My Lamp. She loved that with its rousing chorus of Sing Hosannah. The last one was Colours of Day, another lovely one. Yes she'd feel most uplifted after singing those.

Steve – Reverend Oswald – took his place in the pulpit and welcomed the congregation and her heart did its now customary skip. It was quite acceptable for her to stare at him as he was speaking because everyone else was. He said a welcome prayer then they sang the boring dirge. Someone gave a reading then the sermon followed, focussing on homelessness, which brought the plight of many to mind. Afterwards was the greeting of peace. Lavinia could hardly wait! She did all the polite smiles, greetings, handshakes, some people kissed cheeks, whilst making her way to the front of the church as Steve was making his way to the back. When they greeted each other he took her hand in both of his and squeezed gently but firmly. The pressure was like a warm hug to her hand and it suffused her entire being. They shared a brief smile but she dared not hold his gaze for long for fear of revealing her feelings. Each moved on to the next person then the congregation were seated and invited for Holy Communion.

Lavinia felt an immense gratitude to her parents for getting her confirmed to bring her to this moment. As she stood in the queue to the altar her heartbeat quickened and it was nothing to do with the bread and wine but everything to do with the person ministering it. Did he feel it she wondered or was he just doing his job?

In her turn she knelt at the altar rail, eyes cast down in reverence, hands cupped to receive the wafer. He was moving closer and her heart was racing, then he was with her, placing the wafer in her hands, his hand then resting gently on her head.

"The blessing of God," he said.

She took the wafer into her mouth.

"Amen," she whispered.

She sipped the wine from the chalice as it was offered then rose to return to her seat.

Never had Holy Communion felt so charged. As she walked back down the aisle she felt she ought to apologize to God and to Jesus for the power of her feelings for their minister – was she being sinful to have enjoyed a religious rite so sensuously? But then she still had this notion that God was toying with her emotions. Instead, on reaching her seat, she bowed her head and prayed for the health and safety of her loved ones.

A smile came to her face as she remembered her nephew when he was about four years old at his cousin's baptism. They'd gone for Holy Communion, he'd had a blessing, looked askance at her and when they'd sat down in their pew said to her with the utmost disgust, 'Nobody give me nuffin'!' Precious memories.

The service drew to a close and Steve bid the congregation farewell at the church door. She purposely held back to have a few words alone with him. He did look divine in his work attire. He smiled as she walked towards him and she returned it.

"You made it then," he observed. "What did you think?"

"I enjoyed it very much – well, all except for Make Me a Channel of Your Peace!"

He looked aghast. "Oh, don't you like it?"

"Go on, tell me you love it."

"I do!"

She laughed. "I knew you were going to say that. Lots of people do. I must be missing something. I think it's the most tuneless, boring hymn ever."

"Oh nooo! Don't say that. What hymns do you like then?"

"I loved the other two. I like the lively ones, Shine Jesus Shine, Jubilate."

"I'll remember that. You're confirmed then so you've attended church at sometime."

"Yes, always as a child but as a teen, well I'm a seed that fell by the wayside."

"Perhaps we can tempt you back."

She gave him a coy smile. "Ooh Vicar, isn't tempt a rather naughty word? It brings to mind your adversary."

He winked at her, giving her that delicious heart skip again. "Needs must as they say."

"Well as you're so tempting I may just return, a lamb to the fold as it were."

"You'll be more than welcome. See you soon then?"

"Definitely!"

He watched her walk back to her car. Nice legs in the black tights and black stilettos. He'd noticed them as she'd walked back to her seat after communion. That had been a whole new experience. Never had giving a blessing been so erotic as he'd felt the soft silkiness of her dark hair beneath his hand, heard the sensuality of her whispered 'Amen.' He'd have to seek God's forgiveness for being momentarily distracted from his calling but then God had sent her to him, he felt sure of that, so He wouldn't be displeased – would He? And she'd said she'd come back – definitely! He was getting to like her too much. Was he heading for a fall?

CHAPTER 18

Erica Barber lay on her lonely double bed in abject misery. Curled up into a ball cradling her bump. It should have been the happiest day of her life to date. She and Harvey had been for the twenty week scan to check on the baby's development. All was as it should be; their son was growing well. They'd even seen him kick a leg out. Erica had been fascinated to see the movement of this little life growing inside her. The feel of his movements had been a great source of wonder to her since she'd felt the first one but to actually watch him, know that 'it' was now 'him' was a small miracle. Joy had shone from her face even as she'd looked for emotion in Harvey and found none. Perhaps that wasn't strictly true. What she'd thought she'd seen was fear, as if he'd wanted to run from the room, from her and their baby and she'd found that so hard to bear. She'd wanted to reach out and squeeze his hand, reassure him but she'd known that the last thing he'd wanted was her touch and her shattered heart had spliced yet another fragment.

Walking back to the car she'd tried to get some kind of response from him.

"We can start to think about names now. Had you got any in mind?"

He'd shrugged. "Haven't thought about it."

"Are you pleased it's a boy?"

"Don't mind."

"I'd thought of a couple of names for each, boy or girl. James or Freddie for a boy, Edith or Nancy for a girl. Do you like any of those? Not that girls names matter now."

He'd given a slight shake of his head. "I'm not bothered. You decide."

She'd started to lose patience. "It's for us *both* to decide! Like it or not it's your child too and its name is important – for all of us!"

"I don't care!" he'd snapped. "Choose what you want." He'd stalked off ahead of her and angry then she'd trotted to catch him up.

"Look I'm sick and tired of your attitude to all this. I've tried to be patient, tried to think how you're feeling, it's come as a big shock to us both, but we've both agreed we want this baby even though it was unplanned so the least you could do is show some interest in its sodding name!"

They'd reached the car and he'd opened the door for her, wordlessly slamming it shut as she'd got in.

"Well say something," she'd raged as he'd got behind the wheel, her anger in full flow.

He'd turned sharply to her. "Like what? Do you want me to say everything is OK suddenly and I'm thrilled about all this? Yes you're right, it has come as a shock to us. We'd barely got started. We hadn't thought about the future, whether it would be together or not and now it's got to be whether we like it or not."

"And you're saying not."

"I didn't say that."

"Well what then?"

"I'm saying we hadn't had a chance to make up our minds before they were made up for us."

"But we were good together."

"We were. I really loved you."

"Loved? Past tense?"

"I don't know. I'm confused. I don't know what I feel. I don't *not* love you, but I don't know that I do." He leaned his arms on the steering wheel and ran his hands through his hair. "For fuck's sake I don't know what I feel anymore. Everything is all jumbled up inside and now you're asking me to choose a fucking NAME! Just give me a break will you!"

He started the ignition and reversed out of the car park. The journey home continued in silence.

Now she lay on her bed in the same foetal position as her tiny child, Harvey's words ringing round her head. It was evening but she'd lost track of time. Harvey had gone out with his mates, or would they be people from work? Would Gemma be there? Would they be laughing the way he used to laugh with her before this net had closed over them and bound them together before they'd made the choice themselves? She'd had a bath and now just lay. She couldn't shut out his voice.

Were there threads of hope in there? He'd said he didn't *not* love her, he was confused. People said he'd be OK when the baby was here but what if he wasn't? He hadn't felt the wonder that she'd felt in seeing it – him – on the screen, he wasn't even interested in thinking of a name. How could you not want to think of a name for your child?

Her thoughts churned over and over, chasing each other round her brain like heaving waves, the thread of a positive being swamped by a negative. Self pity started to creep in to add to the mix. Under different circumstances it could have been such a joyous occasion. They could have had a gender reveal party as her sister and brother-in-law had had for their daughter. The pink or blue balloons erupting from the large black baby one as it was popped by the ribbon and lace adorned pin and all the family's cries of delight to know who their newest member would be. Her tears of anguish soaked into her pillow for her precious baby and the blue balloons he'd never have to reveal who he was and she wrapped her arms around him all the tighter to protect him from the disappointments and injustices of the world he was about to enter.

CHAPTER 19

By contrast, Jade and Josh's gender reveal party the previous month, had been a lavish affair. Family and friends had been invited, this baby was Ellis and Donna's first grandchild and although divorced a long time they'd always remained friends. Ellis had been married to Connie for many years and lived at Little Acorn Bird Sanctuary with their daughter Olivia, seven years younger than Jade; Donna had been in a relationship with Theo Stanyer for several years and all were happy and settled.

Josh's family were more complicated having two dads. Adam Hetherington, Dad One, and Nathaniel O'Keefe, Dad Two, who neither had a lot of love for each other but tolerated each other's presence for family occasions, keeping out of each other's way as far as possible. His mother Chloe had been the cause of that bad feeling forming the triangle in their youth but all were civil for the sake of their younger generation.

Liliana and Jake were Josh's sister and brother with their respective boyfriend, wife and children, then came Adam's teenage daughter Ella from his second marriage, whom Josh had always believed to be his sister and had been heartbroken to learn that she wasn't but he didn't love her any the less and they were still close.

The village hall had been bedecked in pink and blue balloons, tablecloths, paper plates and napkins and the parents to be welcomed all of their guests. Everyone was very excited to learn who their new family member was going to be.

Josh had insisted on a canvas of one of his images of Jade being displayed by the food table at the front of the hall, sitting in the garden in a sunset, revealing her bump, the golden light from the sinking sun casting her with an ethereal, maternal glow, her black hair shimmering. He had wanted a different shot which was slightly more revealing but she'd said absolutely not so he'd agreed to this one, in her eyes more tasteful, less intimate. He had agreed in the end that this had the better light.

As soon as all the guests had arrived Jade and Josh had moved to the front of the hall where the large black balloon emblazoned with the swirled white lettering, 'Oh Baby' had sat teasing them all since they'd entered. She'd picked it up and held it aloft, Josh had brandished the giant white pin with its trailing curled ribbons, bore down on it and…

BANG!

Out fell numerous smaller pink balloons and pink and white confetti.

"It's a girl!" went up the cry from the family.

"We're having a girl!" Jade and Josh said to each other, hugging emotionally.

Donna was tearful. "I'm having a granddaughter. Ellis we're having a granddaughter!"

"I know! Our little girl is going to be Mum to a daughter. We are blessed."

They hugged. Donna hugged Theo, Ellis hugged Connie, Olivia went over and hugged her sister.

"I'm going to have a niece!"

"You'll be roped in for babysitting and nappy changing duties! It all goes with the role of auntie," Jade replied.

Ella came over with hugs too. "I'll still have auntie duties won't I Josh?"

"Of course! You're my little sister. Don't think you're escaping the nappy changing."

"I'm so excited! I'll be looking through all of the children's books at work. She'll have her own library in no time."

Ella was a passionate bookworm. At seventeen she was studying English literature at A Level and worked part time in a small bookshop called PageTurners in the neighbouring village of Lower Hayfields. She adored her job and spent much of her spare time there. Adam had bought her a little soft top Mini, she'd passed her driving test first time, and driving to work and college was a joy to her.

PageTurners was a booklovers Heaven. Everything book related could be purchased there. All manner of reading material from classics to modern day fantasy, thrillers and romances plus a bright, colourful children's section, so inviting to young readers. It had a second hand book area and a swap area where people could bring a book to donate, take one away, bring it back when they'd read it and take another if they wished. A little nook was set aside for local authors and all of Celia Wainwright's and Tess Barker's titles, Willows Dip's famous authors books could be found there plus other less well know locals. It gave readers a chance to connect with authors as they would often hold their book launches there, popular events for authors and readers alike where dedicated followers could purchase signed copies. There was also a stationery department selling notebooks and pens of every description, bookmarks and postcards with poems printed on them from competitions run by local libraries. Comfortable armchairs were dotted around for customers to rest on whilst making their choice. Even a tea and coffee machine for those who wanted to stay a while. A bookworm's paradise.

"We'll be bringing her along for lots of visits to Auntie Ella's shop," said Jade. "I think it's so important for children to be introduced to books as early as possible."

"Oh absolutely!" agreed Ella. "Not exactly my shop though! Pauline is the owner. It was always her dream to have a bookshop and it's worked for her. Even though she took a bit of a hit from ebooks her shop is still popular I think because it's so welcoming. We get some tourist trade to the area too."

"Will you stay working there when you finish college? Do it full time?"

"I don't know. I do love it there. It all depends what other opportunities arise but I'm not in a rush to leave. It would depend if she had the hours for me as well."

A distraction took place as Noah, Josh's two and a half year old nephew tore past batting the pink balloons in the air and Daisy his one year old sister who was just taking her first steps toddled after him, interested in the confetti.

"No Daisy don't eat it!" gasped Daddy Jake taking it out of her chubby little hand. "Here let's get you a sandwich."

Adam and Caitlin joined the glowing parents to be. "Have you thought of any names yet?" he asked.

"We can't agree on any can we Josh. We need to get thinking seriously now we're over half way."

"Makes it easier only thinking of girls," added Josh.

Ellis came over and gave his daughter a hug. You're looking great darlin'. How're you feeling?"

"I feel fine Dad thanks. Baby's very active. Seems to wake up when I go to the loo in the night. I hope that's not going to be a habit."

"It probably will for a while. As I recall you weren't a great sleeper at first. It passes though once you get into a routine."

"Let's hope so. I just hope she isn't a screamer!"

The rest of the afternoon passed in merriment and the little girl growing steadily in her mother's womb stretched her tiny limbs in readiness for the outside world.

CHAPTER 20

Lavinia and Jess, one of her florists, were dressing St Luke's church with wedding flowers. Lavinia had suggested to the bride that they would do the church display as part of the package and the starry eyed young woman and her mother had been delighted. In particular they'd liked the arch of white roses over the front two pews for the bridal party to walk through, so that was what had swung it.

Lavinia's increasing visits to St Luke's hadn't gone unnoticed by Jess.

"Bloody hell Lavinia have you found God?"

Lavinia had laughed rather self consciously when she'd said it but Jess had continued with a knowing smile.

"Perhaps it's more finding the handsome vic that's drawn your attention."

"Can't think what you mean," Lavinia had responded with a grin.

"Come off it, you've glowed like a church candle just lately and you can't stop talking about the services you've been attending. It's Steve this, and Steve that."

"That obvious eh."

"Just a bit. I thought you were off men?"

"I am. He's just a pleasant interlude to life."

"Yeah right."

Now they were arranging the flowers for the wedding the following day. Jess had a natural flair, an artist's eye and she and Lavinia often thought as one when it came to floral arrangements. The arch between the pews was coming along well and both were engrossed in their work.

"Would you like a coffee ladies?" Sue the verger called from the vestry.

"That would be lovely thanks," replied Lavinia.

"Come through in about ten minutes then. Steve will be joining us."

Did Lavinia imagine it or did the woman have a twinkle in her eye, and she could feel knowing vibes emanating from her friend and colleague beside her. She just hoped Jess wasn't going to make any suggestive remarks. For herself coffee suddenly held a whole new flavour.

They paused their work and went through to the vestry. Steve was already there and the sun shone even brighter in Lavinia's day for seeing him. Dared she hope it did for him seeing her? He greeted them both with his warm smile and Lavinia felt the observations of the other two women in the room. She was determined not to give anything away! Steve pulled up chairs for them all around the table and Sue placed steaming mugs of coffee before them.

"Help yourselves to sugar and biscuits," she said.

"Have you had a good morning?" Lavinia asked Steve, purposely sitting opposite not beside him, and spooning sugar into her drink.

"Quite pleasant thanks. I've been to the care home to chat to the residents, pray with them, sing a hymn of their choice."

"What did they choose?"

"All Things Bright and Beautiful."

"Nice."

"Reminds me of school," said Jess taking a digestive biscuit from the plate.

"Good or bad memories?" Steve asked.

"Mainly good I'd say. I quite liked school. Loved being in the choir."

"What did you sing?"

"The one that sticks in my mind above others is The Holy City at a concert. Such a powerful chorus."

"Yes one of my favourites too."

"Another one I liked was Duck's Ditty. Such lovely imagery."

"One I remember from school was called Trade Winds," added Lavinia, "about an island with orange trees in the Spanish seas. I always wanted to go."

"And did you?" Steve asked.

She looked downcast. "No, sadly."

"Well you can never say never."

"I suppose not. Never had anyone I wanted to go with." She wished she hadn't said that. It seemed like a leading question although it wasn't a question but as if she was dropping a hint so she changed the subject. "Are you looking forward to tomorrow's wedding?"

"I am!" he replied enthusiastically. "Weddings and baptisms are such joyful occasions."

"Do you ever feel angry as I'm sure some clergy do, that people want a church wedding or to have their children baptised but then don't attend church?"

"How long have you got?"

"As long as you like."

"Mixed feelings. Anything that brings people into church, to God, is good – better if they follow it through. Many people lead good Christian lives by their actions without setting foot in a church, I'm aware of that, just as I'm aware that there are a good many hypocrites who line the pews and would trample on their grandmothers to get what they wanted, but I would like to see some form of feedback from ceremonies. As far as baptisms go it's always important to welcome a child into God's family but again I'd like to see them come to Sunday school. I know families have busy lives now with both parents working but even if they couldn't make it every week just some show of effort when possible would be better than nothing."

"Would you ever refuse to baptise? Some churches only offer a blessing if there's no commitment."

"No I'd never refuse."

"Why not?"

"Because everyone has their beliefs and if someone has a belief in God, has private prayers at home, teaches their child to pray and believe but doesn't have time to attend church then who am I to deny them a baptism?"

"I wish more people thought like you."

He grinned bashfully. "Perhaps I'm a saint." He pushed his chair back and stood up. "Anyway must crack on, I've got a wedding to prepare for. Have you got the Order of Service booklets Sue?"

"I have. Do you want to see them?"

"Yes thanks I'll have a look."

They all got up to return to their work. Every time Lavinia went to the church with flowers or any aspect of her work she always hoped he'd be around but she was often disappointed. Not today though, they'd shared a coffee break with biscuits, broken bread together so to speak.

"He's such a lovely guy isn't he," Jess remarked tucking trailing ivy among the roses. "I can see why you're smitten."

"Yes, I'm a bit too smitten for my liking. It's all getting a bit out of control. I can't get him out of my head."

"Well you'll just have to take it a day at a time."

They continued to work until the arch was completed, white roses interspersed with wispy gypsophila and the contrasting green of the trailing ivy. They stepped back to admire it.

"Doesn't look bad does it," Lavinia said to Jess.

"No I think we've done a good job."

"You've done an excellent job," complimented Steve walking up the aisle behind them. "It looks spectacular. There will be one happy couple tomorrow."

CHAPTER 21

Noel decided it was time to update his wardrobe. He wasn't one for buying clothes, he liked the lived in feel of his old faithful T shirts, jumpers, jeans, joggers. The same with shoes and trainers but perhaps it was time he smartened himself up. Besides, there was good reason on two counts: one to check out Primark to see if Krystina was there and two to look smarter if he did get to see her more often – and then what? Girls had never been interested in him. Lunchtime saw him heading away from Tesco's clothing department and towards the competition.

On the way he saw P.C Jack Adams and his female colleague P.C Lacey Miller. Jack and Lacey were his heroes and saviours along with Steve the vicar. They'd pulled him from the black abyss that had sucked him into the church that day brandishing the knife, all set to kill someone. He hadn't known who, God was going to show him the voice in his head had said. Those three people had come along and saved him. Then they'd introduced him to Brian Welsh, another of his saviours, a counsellor who had slowly over the weeks unravelled the tangled threads of his mind and smoothed them out gently until he could see clearly, and the black depression of his life had once more begun to let in rays of sunlight. Steve had then found him Macy and he had a reason to live again.

"How are you doing Noel?" Jack asked him as he and Lacey approached him with welcoming smiles.

"Great thanks Jack. I've got a dog! Macy her name is."

"Good for you! How did that come about?"

Noel went on to tell him of Syd's death and Steve suggesting he meet Macy and how much she'd changed his life.

"They're great companions, dogs and cats," added Lacey. "I've got one of each, the best of friends to each other and me and my husband. We wouldn't be without them."

"I wouldn't now either," said Noel. "Have you got pets Jack?"

"A dog. Don't want anything else at the moment with a toddler, he's into everything."

They all laughed, bid each other goodbye and went on their way."

Primark was comfortably busy, not too long queues Noel noticed thinking of getting back to work if he bought anything. He wasn't really sure what he was looking for, nothing in particular, anything that took his fancy. He perused the shelves and the rails, had a look at the shoes, finally selecting a blue checked shirt and a light jumper maybe to wear with it. A smart pair of black shoes caught his eye but they'd have to wait until later, he couldn't afford them all at once.

"You've seen something you like then," came a familiar voice, and he turned to see Krystina, his heart lifting along with the smile on his face.

"Yes, my wardrobe is looking a bit neglected. Do you work on this department?"

"No I'm on the ladies department, just passing through on my way back after lunch. Are you on lunch?"

"Yes I'm due back soon. Just going to pay for these first. I'm glad I've seen you. I never asked for your number before."

"OK, get your phone."

She told him and he tapped it in.

"I'm on WhatsApp," she added, "so that's best. Gotta go. Glad I've seen you."

He was too! He'd hardly dared hope he'd see her on his first visit to the store. It was a big place after all and she could be anywhere. He didn't know what part she worked in, if she was on the tills or a department or even the staff canteen, he'd never have seen her then, but luck was on their side and they'd met again, and he'd been brave enough to ask for her number! He'd send her a message tonight.

CHAPTER 22

Erica Barber was browsing the pregnancy shelves in PageTurners, the bookshop in the neighbouring village. So many to choose from, from guides to journals and her heart wrung out at the books for first time Dads. Dare she get one for Harvey? Would it help or hinder the situation? It made her heart pound just to think about it. Everyone trod carefully around him. Even his parents seemed unsure of how to act with him. He was like a firework and you never knew if your next word would light the fuse or not. Best not buy the book. She selected one for herself entitled My First Pregnancy but her heart almost broke when she saw the image on the front cover of an adjacent book of a couple, the expectant Dad behind his partner, his arms around her, hands cradling her growing belly, she leaning back against his supportive strength. How wonderful to have that love. She took her book to the cash desk to pay and noted by the name badge that it was Ella,

Josh's half sister who served her. They only knew each other by sight and just exchanged the necessary pleasantries for the transaction.

Driving home Erica's mood was low and she drove along the lanes on autopilot. Suddenly she was jolted alert by a car overtaking on the opposite side. It had no business overtaking, the lane was far too narrow. It was going to hit her! She braked and swerved right into the hedge and mercifully the overtaking car squeezed in front of the one on the opposite side of the lane, which had also pulled in to allow it to pass. The driver, an elderly man, shrugged to Erica and shook his head and she raised her shoulders and hands to him before they went on their way. No doubt some young hot head driver impatient at seeing someone older in front of him, couldn't wait and thus endangered everyone else's life.

What did she care anyway? She didn't care if she lived or died. Harvey didn't love her or their child. She might end up a single mother. What was the point in going on?

Just then she felt a movement inside her. That little life. 'I'm here,' he seemed to say. 'I'm the point in going on.' With that she knew she had a purpose in life, she needed to live for her son whatever the outcome with his father. She felt the need to talk to her nan and granddad in St Luke's churchyard.

She parked on the edge of the village and walked up to the church. It had rained earlier and puddles shimmered in the afternoon sunlight. Although a churchyard – graveyard – was a sad place of lost loved ones it was also peaceful, allowing you to share thoughts with them. She stopped before their grave.

"Nan, Granddad, I wish you were here. I miss you all the time and especially now. What would you tell me to do about all this? Would you say I was a silly girl to get into this situation in the first place? Perhaps I was but how can I regret my baby? I so want him but I wish his dad did too. Will it all come right do you think?"

She felt tears form in her eyes for her grandparents, for herself, for life. She turned and walked away as Steve was coming out of the church. He noticed her tears and spoke to her.

"Hello Erica. How are you doing?"

She sniffed, wiping her nose on a tissue. "Hello Reverend Steve. I'm just feeling down, as ever. I came to have a chat with Nan and Granddad."

"Did it help?"

She shrugged. "I don't think anything can."

"Can I?"

She gave him a watery smile. "You know my situation don't you, I think everyone does."

"I do yes. What in particular has bothered you today?"

She told him of the close call with the car in the lane. "I wouldn't have cared if I'd died but then I felt the baby move and I knew I had to live for him."

"Is the situation with you and your boyfriend any better?"

"Not really. Harvey is still very distant and withdrawn. I'd thought about going back home to Mum and Dad but my dad said, 'Stick it out Blossom, it'll never work if you run away.'"

"He's right. It's tough for you now but you're stronger than you think and you'll do it for your baby. It seems like this is forever but nothing lasts, everything passes. Once the baby is born your young man may see it all differently, he chose to be there and live with you and his child so that says something. Do as your dad says and stick it out and if you or Harvey either together or separately need to talk, I'm here. We can pray together anytime you like. Would you like to now?"

She nodded, bowed her head and closed her eyes. He laid his hand upon her head.

"Dear Lord, help your child as she carries this new life within her. Give her the strength that she needs and the love and support from those around her. Through Christ our Lord. Amen."

"Amen," repeated Erica.

She raised her eyes and looked into his face. "Thank you Reverend Steve, I needed that."

He patted her shoulder. "Look after yourself and that little one."

As he watched her walk down the path he hoped he'd helped soothe her soul. She was such a lovely girl from a lovely family; she deserved so much better. No-one deserved to go through such anguish especially at such a delicate time of their life. He would keep her in his prayers and hope the Lord would bring guidance to the young couple.

His eyes moved across the village square to where the willow trees dipped their fronds into the waters of the stream giving the village its name and fell upon the brassy blonde hair glittering in the sunlight of Sadie Simcock coiled around someone's husband and he shook his head in despair. It had always been a futile attempt to guide her away from sin. In her eyes she wasn't committing a sin, she was only borrowing someone's man not stealing him. It seemed to be the thrill of the chase or the sense of achievement knowing she could entice him away that seemed to give her the kick. How she could sit in church and pray knowing she had carnal desires for men that she shouldn't Steve could never comprehend. More hypocrisy to line the pews. He wondered what she'd say in the confession box if she were Catholic?

CHAPTER 23

Lavinia looked up from tying the red and white ribbons round a bouquet as the doorbell pinged and her heart gave a delighted skip.

"Hi Steve, what can I do for you?"

"I'd like to order a bouquet for my auntie's birthday please, to be delivered. It's for Friday and I haven't got time to go over on the day."

"Sure. What sort of arrangement were you wanting?"

"Nothing too elaborate, it's not a big birthday yet, seventy something, so just regular flowers. She likes chrysanthemums."

"Yes we can do those. Have a look through the catalogue."

She handed it to him and he browsed through whilst she finished straightening her bow. He made his selection of a yellow and gold bouquet and she took the details.

"Have you got time to come through to the back for a coffee?" she asked.

"That would be lovely thanks. I can squeeze a quick one in."

She led the way into the staff room and put the kettle on.

"Would you like tea or coffee?"

"Don't mind, whatever you're having."

"I'll have coffee. Do you take sugar?"

"One please."

She made the drinks, took them over to the table and produced a packet of chocolate digestives from the cupboard and they both sat down and sipped their drinks.

"Is that OK?" she asked. "Enough milk and sugar?"

He made an OK sign with his thumb and finger. "Perfect. So how have you been?"

"Fine thanks. You?"

"Yes, all good."

"Oh the other day I got snared by the Jehovah's Witnesses at the door."

"Oh dear."

"I don't normally answer if I see them doing their rounds because they keep you for ages don't they – well I don't suppose you know because they wouldn't knock on *your* door – but it was my day off and I was expecting a parcel, bounded to the door like an overexcited Labrador, opened it and there's this smiling elderly couple come to tell me about the devil ruling the earth. My face must have hit the floor."

Steve chuckled over his biscuit. "Go on."

"Did you know that the devil is ruling the earth Steve?"

"I wouldn't have said so but evil is always around. What else did they say?"

"She whipped out her ipad, scrolled through the pages, this whilst he was regaling me with the devil being stripped of his title Lucifer, The Morning Star, The Light, because he isn't, but as we all know he was an angel and cast out from Heaven because he thought he knew better than God so God said 'Well do it your way then.' How do the J.Ws know what God said I wonder? I've never heard that one before."

Steve shrugged, all the time his grin getting wider as Lavinia's tale developed.

"I mentioned a paranormal experience I'd had and they shuddered and recoiled in horror, 'That's the devil's influence,' the old man said. Well, that brought my own image of a mischievous little demon hovering somewhere above my head saying, 'Show them your author friends' books.' I've got several author friends who write fantasy, magical realism, history, about demons, angels, witches, you name it they've covered it and I thought, should I? Perhaps not. I'd never have got rid of them then. They'd have thought I needed my immortal soul saving for sure. Anyway, Little Old Lady had flipped through the ipad and found Joab and she went on about him and angels and well, quite frankly she'd lost me then and I'd lost the will to live."

Steve threw back his head and laughed.

"I tell you Steve I was nearly crying by this point, not to mention almost fainting from hunger. I'm not diabetic but I think there must be some sort of hypoglycaemic issue going on, hence these biscuits, I go all wibbly wobbly if I don't eat regularly, anyway I was praying to anyone who was listening at that point, I didn't even care if it was Satan himself, to make them go away before I expired on the floor. They kept banging on about 'The Truth.' What's with this crap – sorry – about 'The Truth?' Do they think the rest of us are liars or dimwits that don't know what we're talking about? I think it's them with the weird ideas. I've never heard such a load of claptrap in my life. Holy Moley how can anyone be so blinkered! If that isn't brainwashing I don't know what is. Then she says as she hands me her number and The Watchtower – which went straight in the recycling box – if you have any questions just ask! NOOOO!!! If I have any questions I'll ask Jesus myself, I've got Him on speed dial – or I'll ask you. Who do they think they are?"

Steve was by now rolling on his chair and wiping tears from his eyes. "Oh Lavinia I haven't laughed so much in ages."

She grinned in response. "Well if the devil is running the show I think Jesus is doing a pretty good job with my asks of late."

"Oh? And what might they be?"

She tapped the side of her nose. "Ah, now that would be telling. I have a 'To do' list for Him if He's up for it. I always remember my thank yous when He's helped me as well and I try not to keep Him too long because I know He's busy in Ukraine and Gaza but we all have our needs however big or small in the great scheme of world affairs don't we."

"We do."

"Incidentally, what are your opinions on Jehovah's Witnesses?"

He shrugged. "Each to their own. Personally I think they have some strange interpretations of the scriptures. One of our tutors at theological college used to say they were Christians who'd got it wrong and that kind of makes sense to me."

"What's this, 'The Truth,' business? Does it annoy you? It does me a bit in that it implies that we're all a bunch of numbskulls who are wrong – then there's born again Christians! Don't get me started on them! They're a sanctimonious lot if ever there was one. Don't you think?"

"I think there are so many different faiths. We live in a multicultural society and the best we can do is to respect each other's beliefs. Unfortunately not all stick to that principle and that's where the problem lies. Anyway I must be off. Thanks for coffee and biscuits and the laughs! You've certainly brightened my morning. I'll be laughing at that all day!"

She grinned back at him as they walked out into the shop and a rosy glow suffused her soul to know that she'd be in his mind for the remainder of the day. There had been a reason for the J.W visit after all. She mouthed a silent, 'Thank you Jesus.'

CHAPTER 24

It had taken some psyching up for Noel to text Krystina on WhatsApp. He'd never asked a girl out before, in any way, either text or face to face. How did he begin?

After work he walked and fed Macy, had his own dinner but couldn't concentrate on anything. During the walk over the common he'd hoped inspiration might come but it hadn't. They sometimes met Snowball, Macy's cat friend and his owner Alicia – or did cats like to think they owned the humans – but they hadn't today. He wouldn't have shared his dilemma with her, she being several years younger than him and perhaps even then more worldly wise, but he'd thought perhaps a chat with her would have loosened him up a bit, however, no such emotional assistance had transpired and here he sat now staring at WhatsApp on his phone, not daring to scroll to Krystina's name.

'Do it!' commanded the voice in his head, so with shaking

hands he did.

'Hi Krystina, have you been busy today?'

Lame. He deleted it.

'Hi Krystina. How's your day been?'

Better. He clicked the send arrow before he bottled out.

It showed the grey tick, then the second grey tick to say it had reached her phone. He waited for them to turn blue so that she'd picked the message up, his heart thundering against his ribs like the hooves of a raging beast. The ticks turned blue. He waited. She was reading. 'Typing…' appeared beneath her name and the reply arrived.

'Busy. The delivery was late so we were all rushing to get everything out, especially the new lines. How was yours?'

'OK. Usual stuff. Our deliveries were all on time so pretty much routine. I've just walked Macy over the common and had tea.'

'What did you have? Something nice?'

'Sausage, mash and peas, my favourite. What did you have?'

'Mum had done a stew in the slow cooker so it was done for when we got in. We had that with crusty bread, lovely.'

'Sounds it. What are you doing now?'

'I'm going to my friend's in a bit for a chat. What about you?'

'Not much. Just watching TV. What do you think about going out sometime?'

'Yeh great. Where do you want to go?'

'Well what if we could get the same day off and go for a picnic to the park, or would you rather go for a drink in the evening?'

'A picnic sounds lovely if the weather's fine. Shall we try for that then? Synchronize our days off and check the forecast?'

'Sounds great!'

'OK then, I'll let you know when I've spoken with my supervisor.'

He clicked his phone off. The raging beast's hooves in his ribcage had now been replaced by the not unpleasant rhythm of the beat of butterfly wings. He had his first proper date!

CHAPTER 25

Jade was peering discreetly through the front window of her cottage at the house opposite on the new estate where they held the swingers parties. She and Josh watched the ribald goings on with great interest.

"That strange man's hanging around again," she told Josh. "Do you think he's one of them?"

Josh joined her for a sneak peek, sliding his hands around her pregnant belly. "Looks a bit rough. Perhaps he's a dealer. I wonder if they have drugs at these soirées?"

"Never thought of that, I just wondered about all the kinky sex. Come to think of it, I've seen him at the post office. I wonder if he's after Vicki? Perhaps she's recruited him!"

"We'll soon know," Josh nodded towards the window, "here she is."

Sure enough Vicki walked up with her 'Hi Sugar' smile and she and the shifty looking man went inside.

"He's not a nice sort of person is he," Jade mused. "Nothing you could put your finger on – ha, mind you I bet she'll find something to put her finger on – he's just got that hard look about him hasn't he. I don't like hard people, I like nice people."

"Me too. Well we're nice people aren't we so that will follow. I wonder if hard people like hard people or if they want to beat them up? I wonder if he'll be tying Vicki to the bed and if she'll enjoy it?"

Jade turned in his arms with a seductive gleam in her eye. "I might enjoy it if you tied me to the bed." She trailed a finger down his chest to the belt on his trousers.

"Really!"

"Well, perhaps not tied but I like it when you photograph me."

Desire glowed in his eyes at the joining of his two passions, his lover and his photography. "Wait right there."

He returned with his camera.

She licked her lips seductively whilst unbuttoning her shirt to reveal the white lace bra. She cupped her breasts and raised her eyes to his. The shutter on his camera whirred getting every movement as she shed the shirt and unclasped the bra, letting it fall to the floor. He loved her pregnant body cradling their daughter and particularly her breasts preparing to nourish her. He was unable to resist caressing them gently, putting aside the camera, kissing them, kissing a burning path the length of her body as she moaned with pleasure. He was always gentle with lovemaking thinking of the baby but his senses were on fire, he'd never found her more sexy and desirable than in her current state as a woman.

Afterwards they lay together, languid in the afterglow.

"It always turns me on thinking of what they're up to over the road," said Jade idly stroking his chest.

He grinned wickedly at her. "I know and I love it. I'm always happy to see one of their gatherings because I know the effect it has on you."

"Don't you get aroused thinking about it?"

"I get aroused thinking about you, especially as you are. I think

I'll keep you barefoot and pregnant."

"I'm so glad you do. It must be so awful for Erica not to feel attractive and sexy at such a time mustn't it."

"It must. I can't understand though how any man wouldn't find his pregnant partner attractive and sexy. It's ultimate womanhood, the height of femininity. To me you've never looked more desirable. He must be mad not to see it in her."

"Not all men are as soulful as you Josh. There's a deep sensitivity to you that some men lack. I'm just so happy that we came together and after we'd grown up together and never suspected anything between us. Strange how it happened wasn't it."

He twisted her long hair round his finger. "You're such a forward woman Jade Watson, seducing a young boy like me."

She slapped him playfully. "Oh I did not! I rescued you from that slag you were hanging round with, and I never knew what a fantastic kisser you were."

"Am I still a fantastic kisser?"

The teasing passion mounted between them again.

"Possibly. You'll have to try me with another so I can give an accurate assessment."

CHAPTER 26

Alexa Barber had taken daughter Erica pram shopping.

"Dad and I will buy you the pram as we did for Helena and Jake but you choose; we'll go together. They always used to say it was bad luck to have the pram in the house before the baby was born so Dad and I will pick it up and keep it at ours. How does that sound?"

Erica had shrugged despondently. "Whatever."

"Chin up," her mother had said, "it'll be good to go and choose."

Now here they were in Pramworld and Erica had cheered up considerably on the mother/daughter shopping expedition.

"Harvey's parents are buying the cot aren't they," Alexa said, "his mum messaged and said she'd suggested it."

"Yes, and there's a changing unit with drawers underneath to match so I'm getting that. It'll all just about fit in my room. I've made space in my wardrobe for clothes on hangers and there's a pod that fits onto the side of my bed for him to sleep next to me when he's tiny that I'll get."

"How are you doing for essentials, cot sheets, vests etc?"

"OK. I've got a couple of packs of vests, one white, one blue, and a few pairs of cot sheets."

"Let's have a look in here today to see if there's anything else you need but we'll sort the pram out first, that's the priority."

They'd already looked in a few other places and compared prices and brands and had narrowed their choice down to the Mamas and Papas travel system and the Oyster.

"So hard to choose," said Erica. "I love them both."

"What about colour?"

"Well I like the Oyster Champagne."

"Perhaps that's the decider then?"

Erica swung from one to the other. "Yes I think you're right, I'll go for the Oyster. I could procrastinate forever, need to make a decision and they'll both do the same job."

"OK let's go and see if there's anything else we need before we order it then we can pay all at once."

They wandered round the store looking at all the baby requisites.

"Have you got a nappy bag?" asked Alexa.

"No not yet, haven't really looked."

"You'll need that for when you go out. Let's see what they've got."

They looked through a selection and Erica chose one a similar colour to the pram and opened it up. "Lots of pockets inside for nappies, wipes and stuff, bottles and spare outfits. Looks a good one doesn't it."

"Shall we have that then?"

"Yes I think so thank you. It's very kind of you to pay for all this Mum."

"Nana treats. I love it. Come on we'll make our way to the till and order the pram."

"Exciting isn't it!" exclaimed Erica. "I haven't felt this excited about anything all the way through. Well I was excited about the scans but Harvey being like he is took the shine off it."

"No better?"

Erica shook her head.

Alexa squeezed her hand. "We won't think about him today. This is our day. We'll enjoy a bit of retail therapy for this little man." She patted Erica's tummy.

Once the pram had been ordered and their items paid for they headed back to the car.

"Let's go somewhere for lunch," suggested Alexa starting the ignition. "All this spending has given me an appetite."

CHAPTER 27

The tuners were in church tuning the organ and Steve never ceased to be amazed at the technology, they even used a laptop as part of the tuning process to get the tone right. There was also the practical aspect of checking the air supply. Every pipe had to be listened to to make sure they all played at the correct volume; the tip of the pipe needed to be closed or opened to make it louder or softer. Even the tuners were in tune with each other! The pair seemed to have a sixth sense when working together.

Depending on his work schedule Steve couldn't always be around during the whole of this procedure but he liked to put in an appearance for some of the time because it fascinated him and he loved to hear the finished effect. He always marvelled at their expertise and usually found himself humming along to the tune of a hymn after it.

He tried never to get in their way; there was nothing worse than someone breathing down your neck when you were trying to work, he usually got on with some menial task within the church, straightening this, tidying that, making sure all the kneelers were in place.

Today he sat in one of the back pews going through his diary. Summer was drawing its blinds and harvest time would soon be upon them. It was a particularly enjoyable time, celebrating God's bounty. The school assemblies were fun, the children bringing along their gifts to be distributed to more needy people. When he was a boy growing up it had always been the elderly of the neighbourhood. Now foodbanks had some donations. Schoolboy memories came back of knocking on doors which were answered by grey curly haired grannies, grateful for a tin of soup and a packet of biscuits and he'd felt the satisfaction of giving from that young age. Perhaps it had kick started his calling into the church.

He couldn't pinpoint an exact moment when he'd wanted to become a vicar. God hadn't appeared to him in a blinding flash of lightning or anything so dramatic, it had just crept up on him quietly like a secret admirer, drawing him to her. He'd always felt at home in a church, loved the peaceful, calming atmosphere, that ethereal ambience. His parents had been amazed but supportive. His father was a joiner, his mother a seamstress and they'd been proud when telling people their son was attending theological college. It had been eight years before he'd been ordained and he'd had a couple of parishes before coming to Willows Dip but once here he'd wanted to stay. That was unusual. Most clergymen moved around to new parishes but he hadn't wanted to leave. He'd met Lisa, they'd had the boys and were happy to stay put.

He'd seen the villagers through many joys and tragedies. A vicar's role was to give comfort where needed. Funerals, weddings, baptisms were regular events along with charity work, school visits, care home and hospital visits, giving last rites, all were a part of his calling. Some events stuck in his mind more than others though.

One such event was the terrible car accident that had resulted in Adam Hetherington losing a leg, then married to Chloe O'Keefe with Jake a baby. Chloe and Jake had escaped with barely a scratch but Adam's leg had been trapped and had to be amputated. His heart had gone out to him – to them as a family – and soon after Chloe had met Nathaniel O'Keefe and their marriage had failed. During that time Chloe had come to him with a question about attending a spiritualist church and he hoped he'd given her good advice. As a Christian minister of course he had a belief in Heaven and a life beyond earthly life but whether it was right to dabble in it was another matter.

Another parishioner whose troubles he'd felt had been Connie Watson. She'd lost her first husband Kev in the war in Kosovo and suffered a very tough time before she opened Little Acorn Bird Sanctuary. Life had improved for her after meeting Ellis but her beloved grandmother Alice Miller, affectionately known by her as Nana Crashitt had been murdered by conmen calling at her house. Poor Connie had had more than her fair share of emotional trauma to deal with. Although she hadn't sought him out with her troubles he'd prayed for her and asked for God's blessings and guidance for her.

Years later Willows Dip had seen the discovery of an unidentified body on the common and following that had come the Covid 19 pandemic that had affected everyone, some losing their life to it, some having their life changed by it, but life went on, babies were born, people died and the role of a clergyman was always fulfilled.

A chord from the newly tuned organ pulled him out of his reverie and he realized he'd got nowhere with his diary. The king of digression he was. His thoughts always ran on from one track to another. He stretched, closed the diary and went to get some proper work done.

CHAPTER 28

After the abysmal summer of almost relentless rain since July, the fourth of September was kind to Noel and Krystina for their first date. The sun beamed down on them from pellucid blue skies and it mirrored their delightful anticipation of an afternoon to be spent together.

They met at noon at the park gates and Noel took her hand instinctively – it just happened; he didn't plan it or think about it, their hands were drawn together as if by a higher power. She looked beautiful, wearing a yellow and white sundress which set off her long blonde hair, with tied shoulder straps, no bra he noticed and felt his pulse quicken. Only wearing light make up with a touch of pale lipstick; he felt the urge to kiss it off. Later he hoped. He'd chosen a short sleeved cotton shirt, blue and white check and after some thought he'd gone for light summer trousers as opposed to shorts which he'd felt were too casual. They'd both contributed to the picnic which they carried in backpacks.

They made small talk as they walked around the lake and fed the ducks. A family of swans with well grown cygnets came along for a snack, and a single white goose.

"He looks lonely," mused Krystina, making sure he had some of her wholegrain bread. "Do you think he's lost his mate?"

"I don't know," Noel replied. "I've often seen geese such as him on their own so perhaps they're not as gregarious as the Canada geese."

"Maybe. I hope he finds a companion."

"Shall we look for somewhere to sit for our picnic?"

She nodded. "Better move away from here a distance or we'll be sharing it with these!"

They walked a little way further on and found a sunny, secluded spot.

"Here?" they suggested simultaneously, and laughed. Decision made they sat down on the grass and undid their backpacks. Krystina pulled out a red and white gingham cloth that she laid out for them to put their packets of sandwiches on.

"What have you brought?" she asked him.

"I did some ham and some cheese. Do you like them?"

"Yes thanks, love both. I did egg, and Mum baked us chocolate muffins – she was excited for me – do you like them?"

"Yes, delicious. I brought us San Miguel to drink. You said you liked it."

"I do! It all looks gorgeous doesn't it. Isn't this exciting!" She clapped her hands like a little girl at a birthday party and he found it most endearing and wanted to hug her to him and kiss her there and then but they must eat first.

"Lovely. Let's tuck in, I'm starving."

Initially they ate in silence to take the edge off their hunger but presently Noel asked, "What does your mum do when she isn't making muffins for us?"

"She's a supervisor at Morrison's."

"Ah, our competition."

"Yeah."

"What department?"

"Tills."

"Has she been there long?"

"Years. She started as cashier, went part time when I was young then applied for the supervisor's post when she and Dad split up when I was twelve."

"Why did they split up? Sorry I'm being nosy. Don't answer that."

"No it's fine. He met someone else. Ran off with his own supervisor in the shoe shop where he worked. Mum always suspected there was something between them but he denied it but she'd been right."

"Do you get on with him – and her?"

"Yeah, OK – ish. He's still my dad."

"Do you like her or forgive her for taking him away?"

"I don't give it much thought. I neither like nor dislike her. It is what it is."

"Do they have any children?"

"No thank goodness. That would have put a whole new complexion on matters. She's got a son from her first marriage."

"Do you get on with him?"

"Where I have to. We're all very civil but I don't think any of us would be big buddies; we tolerate each other."

"Is your mum with anyone?"

"No, never seems to meet the right person. She did like someone but he was married so all they ever did was chat. There have been a couple of men interested in her but she didn't return the interest. I think she prefers her own space. Anyway what about you? You never say anything about your dad."

"Bad man. We escaped him when I was in nursery school. My mum moved area so he wouldn't be able to find us. I don't remember anything about him and don't want to."

He picked up his beer and took a drink and she did the same. Putting their bottles down he leaned forwards and reached for her.

"Let's not talk about our parents, we're here for us."

He put his hand behind her head and drew her face towards his, their lips meeting as he'd dreamed of these last weeks. He needn't have worried because their kiss was the most natural movement in the world. He felt her arm slide up his back and the arms they were propped up on relaxed as they lay down on the cool grass. His hand slid over her bare shoulders, the feel of her warm skin beneath his fingers exciting him. He dared skim over her breast feeling the softness with lack of a bra through the thin cotton of her dress and his senses were on fire. He wanted to linger there, caress that firm swell in his hand, knead it gently in his fingers but he held back for fear of scaring her off; he didn't want to rush anything because he knew without a doubt that he wanted to see her again and again and again. Instead he let his hand stray to safer territory, the smooth silkiness of her shoulders, enjoying the feel of her fingers running through his hair, her other hand caressing the taut muscles of his back.

How long they kissed neither knew but then they just lay in each other's arms. He drew sensuous circles on her shoulder with his finger, she slid her fingers between the buttons of his shirt to tease the hair on his chest. They just lay.

As afternoon drew to tea time they moved to sit up and pack the remains of their picnic away.

"It's been the most heavenly afternoon," she said placing a kiss on his lips. "Thank you for asking me."

He returned the kiss. "Thank you for accepting. It's been so good to be with you. Do you want to go and see a film next time?"

"Love to."

CHAPTER 29

Raining again," observed Jade looking out of the back bedroom window where she and Josh were decorating the nursery.

"When will it ever stop?" he asked rhetorically, wielding the roller of pink paint over the wall.

"It'll be a quiet day in the post office for the underworld clientele withdrawing cash for their 'supplies' for the weekend."

"What makes you say that?"

"It's what Sticky Vicki said once when I was in and commented on it being quiet. 'Oh they won't come out today Sugar, they're like rats, don't come out when it's raining, that is unless they're desperate for another pipe.' I wonder if they all share a pipe or two at the soirées across the road?"

"Ha ha that's funny. Yes it makes you wonder doesn't it. Sticky Vicki ha ha, suits her."

"I mentioned the illicit goings on over there to Reverend Steve. I wonder what he thinks of it all? Perhaps he thinks they're beyond saving and it's Lucifer's den of sin. Then there's the local police P.Cs Jack Adams and Lacey Miller. They must be aware of it."

"Perhaps it's just a harmless get together. Maybe they've checked it out when we haven't been watching. I don't think it'll necessitate the drug squad will it."

"Probably not. They're not doing anything illegal are they, just a bunch of kinky old farts having a good time."

"It'd be fun though wouldn't it if the police turned up. Could you just imagine? I wonder what erotic sights they'd see, what states of undress people would be in? Ha they wouldn't need their own handcuffs, I bet there'd be a few pairs in use already!"

"Yeah it'd be quite a show wouldn't it; make interesting viewing. Shame we couldn't have Xray vision and see through the walls. Changing the subject, are we settled on Marnie Elise for the baby's name?"

"I think so don't you, and your dad will like Elise being the female form of Ellis."

"Do you mind that there's no nod to your family?"

"No. I think we have to go with what sounds right for us don't we. I wouldn't feel right having Chloe after my mum and we haven't got Donna after yours. My two dads Nathaniel and Adam, what would that be, Natalie and Eve? No, I think we're right as we are, go with what fits for us."

"Yes I think so and I like Elise, Marnie first."

"I can't wait to meet her."

"Me neither. Not too long to go now. I wonder if she'll be early or late?"

"She could be a Christmas baby."

"We'll just have to wait and see won't we."

CHAPTER 30

Harvest was always a busy time for Steve but a time that he enjoyed immensely. On Friday he'd led the assembly at Cranberry primary school; so uplifting to hear the children's voices blending as they sang 'Come Ye Thankful People Come,' from the words on the whiteboard screen at the front of the hall. It was all new to the reception class children who had only been at the school for a few weeks so they were led by the older children, although they'd have practiced the hymn in their classes beforehand. The Y6 children knew it well. All had brought food for the needy; most would be going to the local food bank, and there was a good display to be packed up later. It was rounded off with a prayer of thanksgiving for God's bounty.

Sunday had seen the harvest service in church. Lavinia had suggested asking the parishioners to bring flowers from their gardens and hedgerows to adorn the church and give it a natural ambience. There was a good mix of hips and haws with cultivated blooms and foliage, a varied selection. She had given her time to advise on decoration and arrangements and Steve had kept space in his diary for when she was there, to take part in the activity. He wouldn't allow the enjoyment he found in her company to become a conscious thought; that would be straying into dangerous territory. Maybe there would come a time when he'd have to listen to that inner voice, the voice of his soul that seemed to be drawing him towards her, but not just yet. For now he'd just go along with the pleasure he got when she was near. In weaker moments, in repose, he wondered if she felt it too, this companionship, this compatibility between them. He'd allow his thoughts to run on for a time, think of her a little, but not too much, he'd been on his own a long time and he didn't know if he wanted someone in his life – ever. He didn't know her circumstances and he wouldn't ask. That would imply interest and he couldn't allow that. No, best not think too much. File her away in his mental cabinet of pleasant encounters.

The Sunday service had gone well as it usually did and now it was Monday, the evening of the harvest supper in the village hall. Once again Lavinia had volunteered her help and Steve had felt that flutter of joy that he refused to let have headway. All the same he couldn't keep from gravitating towards her or delighting in that frisson of electricity if their hands brushed when exchanging some item or other.

The Simcock sisters were holding sway in the kitchen, bickering over the stew.

"Keep stirring that Sadie!" snapped Lydia. "Don't let it boil over."

"I am! I was just thinking about the man in the chemist."

"Ye Gods you're always thinking about some man, usually somebody else's. Whose husband is this? I hope he's better than the last one, his eyes were too close together. Anyway what do you want with a man at your age? Old fool."

"Well why shouldn't I? Connie Watson's husband's nice."

"That's always been your trouble, always wanting what somebody else has got. 'Do not covet thy neighbour's wife' – or husband in your case – and watch that stew! I've told you to keep stirring it!"

Steve and Lavinia exchanged a smirk. He always felt rather sorry for Sadie for all her maneating ways. Lydia was a proper crosspatch, always criticising her; he didn't know how she put up with the constant put downs.

"It smells delicious Sadie," he remarked. "Have you made it?"

"Oh no Vicar. I prepped the veg, Lydia cooked it. I can't be trusted with the cooking; I burn everything."

"The vicar doesn't want to know all that!" barked Lydia. "Look, you're boring the pants off him."

"She's not – you're not, I assure you," Steve added to Sadie. "You're doing a grand job, carry on." He refrained from patting her on the shoulder lest he be added to her list of possibilities. He didn't think as he often did that his dog collar would be enough protection should Sadie get any such notion to get closer to God in a different way. "Now, would you like Lavinia and I to take the bread rolls out onto the tables?"

"If you would please," said Lydia gathering the small baskets and putting the rolls into them, already prepared with paper napkins inside them. She then began ladling the stew into bowls – something else she wouldn't trust her sister with.

As the food was transferred to the main hall from the kitchen the villagers all tucked into the wholesome autumn fare and complimented the cooks. More volunteers were on tea and coffee making duties, juice for the children. Once the food was cleared away and the dishwasher stacked and programmed the quiz got underway. This was always devised by Steve and Sue, the verger with more than a little help from the Internet and TV. People usually worked in teams from their tables with a box of chocolates as the prize for the winner. The fun part came with the reading out of the answers.

"Question ten," continued Steve, "what isn't an animal. 1. A Leonberger, 2. An Axolotl, 3. A Lichen, 4. A Zebra."

Everyone waited, some chewing the end of their pens.

"Answer, number three, A Lichen, it's neither plant nor animal. It's an organism, a combination of an algae and a fungus."

"Oooh," wailed little Tommy Brown. "I put Leonberger."

His mum laughed. "A Leonberger is a big dog."

"I didn't know. I thought it was summat eat."

Everyone within earshot roared with laughter and Tommy scowled. The winner was duly announced, the prize awarded and the evening drew to a close, the villagers filing out into the darkness, leaving the volunteers to tidy up. Tablecloths were shaken and folded ready to be washed, tables stacked away, the floor swept. The village hall was left as neat and tidy as it was found ready for its next use. Everyone said goodnight leaving Steve to lock up.

"It's been a great night," Lavinia said as she waited for him to pocket the keys. "I can't think why I've never been to one before."

They stood close in the entrance porch, facing each other, their eyes large with only the light from the streetlamp.

"I'm glad you enjoyed it," he answered smiling down at her. "They're usually fun."

"Don't you ever run out of ideas for the quiz?" Her heart was beating wildly, they'd never stood this close and under the duvet of darkness; she could feel the soft caress of his breath warm and whisper light on her cheek.

"Not often, the Internet is full of them and there are plenty of snippets on TV."

A couple walked past them on the street. "Goodnight Vicar," they called taking his attention and the spell was broken.

"Goodnight," he replied, then to Lavinia, "Well, goodnight then. See you at Sunday's service?"

"Yes, I'll be there. Goodnight."

She walked towards her car with the lead weight of disappointment replacing the light flight her heart had felt moments before. They'd been so close until that couple walked past. Were his flock always going to be there? Would he ever kiss her?

CHAPTER 31

The next service was a blessing for pets. A very popular addition to the church calendar, everyone loved to bring their beloved furry family members to have the vicar's hand laid upon their head to impart God's blessing. From small children with their gerbils, hamsters, rabbits, mice, birds, to larger animals, cats and dogs, sometimes ponies and donkeys had waited patiently in the churchyard for Reverend Steve to go out to them. Connie Watson usually brought one of her birds from the sanctuary as a representative for them all. Her beloved Nana, affectionately known as Nana Crashitt for her cavalier driving skills had had a parrot called Bramer for many years whom she'd brought along. Bramer had a colourful vocabulary and had the congregation in hysterics and Nana red faced as he mimicked the sound of the doorbell and added, 'Who the fuck is that now?' No-one could ever have imagined Nana – Alice to give her her proper name – swearing, she was such a dear sweet old lady, called everyone, 'Ma darlin' but where else could the bird have heard it? Nevertheless he came for his blessing but never mimicked 'Amen.' Both now gone and sadly missed.

Chloe and Nathaniel O'Keefe had come along with Josh and Jade to bring Izzy, Josh's border collie for her blessing. When covid had struck and Josh had isolated at Jade's mother Donna's home, then when he and Jade had bought their own home, all had felt it unfair to uproot Izzy. Although she'd missed Josh dreadfully her home was his former home, with Chloe, Nathaniel and Liliana so that's where she'd stayed. Now middle aged she'd adapted to the changes.

Chloe wasn't an animal person but she liked to be with her family, plus she didn't like to have Nathaniel wandering alone among throngs of women. She'd always been well aware of his sexual magnetism and though they'd remained faithful to each other and she trusted him implicitly, it was other women she didn't trust. She'd never missed lustful, lascivious looks devouring her husband by more predatory females and with the likes of Sadie Simcock on the loose, always on the lookout for a lone man, Chloe would tolerate the animal population to defend what was hers.

The church began to fill up and wuffs, miaows and squawks echoed round the walls. Just then a couple in their forties were dragged in by an exuberant black labradoodle who cocked his leg on the door post making his presence known. So excited was he at the sight of all the other dogs that he repeated the action all up the aisle, much to the chagrin of the red faced woman hanging onto his lead for dear life.

"Zak! Stop! Bad dog!"

She came face to face with Reverend Steve looking pristine in his white robe and blushed further.

"Oh I'm so sorry Vicar, he's pissed up every pew. He's such a naughty boy. We can't take him anywhere. Zak! No! Not again!"

Steve grinned. "Not to worry, we're always prepared for small accidents."

"Small accidents! He's scent marked the whole church! Made it his own. Oh I knew we shouldn't have brought him," she wailed turning to her husband who looked as though he'd like to crawl under one of the kneelers and vanish.

Steve patted both of their arms. "Don't worry. He deserves a blessing as much as everyone. Look, Sadie is here with the mop and disinfectant already."

Sure enough Sadie appeared like a ministering angel wielding said piece of equipment with great aplomb, smiling at all the men, never letting her humble task stop her hunt for fresh meat. She lingered a little longer by Nathaniel's pew earning her a glare from Chloe that washed right over her and she carried on unabashed.

Steve was pleased to see Lavinia in church with her niece who she introduced as Minnie.

"And who's this you've brought to be blessed Minnie?" he asked peering into the cage that she carried oh so carefully.

"He's my gerbil Bruno, like in Encanto," answered the little girl confidently.

Steve had no idea about Encanto other than it was a Disney movie but he didn't show his ignorance. "He looks very sleepy, I don't think he'll be any trouble do you?"

"Oh no, he's very good."

He and Lavinia exchanged a smile as she took Minnie and found a seat.

Noel had come along with his little dog Macy as had Alicia Rose the young Australian girl with Snowball her white cat and Macy's friend. They'd arranged to meet each other for the service when they'd seen each other out walking as an extra treat for their pets. Macy was seated on Noel's knee and such was the animals' exuberance at seeing each other he also had Snowball as he wound round a delighted Macy and the two were in real danger of toppling off onto the floor. Once their initial greeting was over they settled down together in a furry bundle and Noel felt honoured that the two animals were so comfortable with him.

Once everyone including the excitable Zak were settled after a fashion the service commenced. It was very informal and of course the hymn had to be All Things Bright and Beautiful, All Creatures Great and Small. The friendly neighbourhood ginger and white cat, Marco, who visited everyone and had a treat at his various diners before returning to his comfortable home to snooze and recharge his batteries for his next patrol, gave a warning hiss at the overfamiliar Zak before turning his back on him and nonchalantly washing behind his ears from the safety of his mum's lap.

One by one the animals were trooped up to the altar for their blessing before departing for some lunch. Steve smiled to himself. It had been a heartwarming and entertaining service. A pity he'd not had chance for a proper chat to Lavinia but there'd be other days.

CHAPTER 32

Noel had cleaned the house to within an inch of its life; Krystina was coming over for a pizza and to watch a film and staying the night. They both knew what that meant and had touched on the subject before but he hadn't been quite brave enough to confess that it would be his first time, or ask if it was hers. He suspected not but again he hadn't dared delve too deeply, it would only have added to the anxiety and he didn't want anything to spoil it. Since their picnic their passion had developed and it had only been a matter of time before they were both ready to take their relationship to the next level. Now the evening was here.

He'd showered, washed and styled his hair, shaved, hoped he hadn't gone overboard on the Lynx Africa, chose a shirt he knew was a favourite of hers, lit scented candles in the living room and just had those and the soft light from the lamp to illuminate.

The doorbell rang promptly at 7.30.p.m and he opened it to let her in. She looked beautiful as she always did in his eyes, smart red coat setting off her blonde hair, which was as sleek and silky as satin. As he closed the door behind her and helped her off with her coat he noticed the fine bones of her shoulders beneath the red and white checked dress. Black tights and shoes completed the outfit and he told her how beautiful she looked, dropping a quick kiss on her lips.

"Thanks," she smiled, "you don't look half bad yourself. My favourite shirt I see." She trailed a hand across his chest sending a flare of desire through him which he quelled until after they'd eaten.

"I've ordered the pizzas, they won't be long. What film shall we watch?"

"Let's go for something romantic. How about The Notebook?"

"OK whatever you like. Oh, pizzas are here."

He answered the door to collect their food, brought a bottle of Prosecco and two glasses from the kitchen and they made themselves comfortable in front of the TV. Macy after having greeted Krystina with the usual enthusiasm that she did on walks was happy to settle in her bed and snooze.

Initially they ate and concentrated on the film as the elderly man in it reminisced about his youth with his love; she by now didn't know who he was, and the scenes took them back to being young lovers.

"So sad isn't it," murmured Krystina. "Do you think it will ever happen to us?"

Noel moved the empty pizza boxes onto the coffee table and pulled her close. "Who can say? It's a long way off isn't it. We've got a lot of life to live if all goes well."

She snuggled into him as the film continued. When it finished her eyes were misty. "Such a beautiful story."

"It was."

A tear rolled down her cheek and he brushed it away, kissing her tenderly. Her arms wound round his neck as she pulled him down to her. The moisture in her eyes made them large and luminous and she'd never looked more desirable lying seductively beneath him. He undid the buttons of her dress and slid his hands inside feeling the now familiar curve of her breast and heard her gasp as he increased the pressure. He felt her legs part as he kissed her neck and moved between her thighs. Her hands undid his belt and he knew a moment's panic that he'd be unable to wait but they were both eager for each other. They removed clothes in a frenzy of hot, passionate kisses, hands discovering hitherto secret places and their oneness was the most natural joy in the world.

Afterwards they lay spent, sweat glistening on their naked bodies in the candle and lamp light. He wanted to ask her if it had been OK but he didn't want to sound clichéd. He also wanted to know if was her first time. He didn't think it was as there had been no resistance but he wasn't experienced enough to know and he didn't want to reveal that fact. She saved him the trouble.

"That was amazing," she whispered caressing his chest.

He glowed with pride, like being awarded the greatest prize at school but he didn't want to reveal his elation lest it also reveal his inexperience.

"Was it your first time?" she added.

That snatched the prize away.

"Could you tell?"

"No, not by just now, you were a superb lover, tender and hot in all the right places, but you've never spoken of anyone else."

Oh superb! That swelled his ego again.

"There's never been anyone else. I've never met anyone I've got on with or liked enough or just gelled with. I always thought I'd be alone. Then I met you – in a graveyard of all places! What about you? Was it your first time?"

She lowered her eyes and shook her head as if regretfully.

"Have you been in a relationship before?"

"Not as such. I went out with someone who wanted to sleep with me, I didn't want to but gave in in the end to shut him up. I didn't enjoy it and finished with him after that. I regretted it really.

Losing your virginity should be something special, like we just had. He spoilt that."

"Well we can make up for it now. I know it's not that first time but this is our first time so it's special for us both isn't it."

"Yes we could look at it like that. Was it all you imagined it would be?"

"And more. It would be with the right person wouldn't it, and you're the right person. I love you Krystina."

Here eyes reciprocated before her lips did. "And I love you Noel."

CHAPTER 33

The congregation of St Luke's parish church led by Reverend Steve had fallen into line behind the Salvation Army band to join the procession to the Cenotaph in Hartford town centre for the Remembrance Day service. The rector Keith Simpson would lead the service and Steve's more personable character would lift the malodourous atmosphere cast by his superior.

Lavinia walked a little way behind thinking how sexy Steve looked with his white vestment billowing in the breeze. Should she feel guilty having lustful thoughts about the vicar? Whatever. God had led her to this she was sure of it so how could He disapprove? She always wanted to be close to Steve but didn't want to make it obvious to either him or his congregation. Her own friends and staff at the florist were well aware of her thus far thwarted longings concerning the good man of God and she didn't want to look a complete lovesick fool in the eyes of the whole village. She battled with her emotions constantly. She had no idea of his feelings towards her. He liked her, she felt sure of that, but was it anymore than any of his parishioners? The closest they'd ever got was the evening of the harvest supper as he was locking the village hall, then that couple had walked past and called goodnight to him. Would he have kissed her if they hadn't? She could have cursed them but that would have been wrong. Now all of a sudden she was consumed by the feelings of good against evil – well perhaps not evil but sinful. Since when had she become a God botherer? 'Since you had designs on His servant!' came one of her inner voices that were a part of her torment.

It drove her mad wondering how he felt about her. They got on well together, laughed at the same things, talked easily together. He often asked if she'd be at services. 'They're not dates though, stupid woman,' spat the more peevish inner voice. No they weren't dates, she knew that but it warmed her soul that he wanted her as part of his congregation. Their eyes often locked as he delivered his service and she felt the butterflies flutter in her stomach. Was she right to keep waiting and hoping that something might develop between them? What if it did? Where could or would it lead? Her thoughts that were always twenty leaps ahead hadn't got round to figuring that one out.

Another pair of adoring eyes fixed on Reverend Steve were those of Noel as he held Krystina's hand in the procession. She was wearing the red coat that he found so attractive on her and she noticed how his eyes gravitated to the vicar.

"You're very fond of the Reverend aren't you," she observed.

"He saved me," Noel answered. "Him and P.C. Jack Adams. I was in a very dark place after I lost Mum. I wanted to kill someone to avenge her death and those two got me on the right path."

"It must have been a tough time for you."

"It was."

"Are you over it now?"

"I still have bad days, spells of anxiety, I wonder if I always will.

My childhood with an abusive father made me anxious as well. I've always had panic attacks."

"I've never seen you have one."

"I've learned to control them with the help of the counsellor through meditation and medication although I'm off the medication now, since meeting you and I see the counsellor less."

"Have I helped you then?"

"You've brought me happiness and contentment and now love." He squeezed her hand. "I'd never expected to find any of it and I do sometimes have flutters of panic about losing you and it scares me."

She returned the squeeze on his hand. "You won't lose me, I promise."

"You might have an accident like my mum did."

"I'll be very careful. Let's not think about that and pray to your vicar's God that neither of us do."

The procession reached the Cenotaph and everyone found a place. Keith loomed Lurch-like beside Steve, a complete contrast to the handsome profile. The band was silent as the service commenced before striking up again for the first hymn, 'I Vow to Thee My Country.'

Such a moving hymn and Lavinia felt a tug at her heartstrings remembering all the young servicemen and women who had given their lives in wars and conflicts. She couldn't take her eyes off Steve and he must have felt them as he looked her way and they exchanged a brief smile.

Prayers were said, wreaths laid and the two minutes silence observed at 11 a.m. Lavinia thought of her own family who'd been involved in WWII and the many stories she'd heard from grandparents, aunts, uncles and parents. Such terrible times and terrible times had happened in many ways since through terrorism: 9/11, 7/7, the troubles with the I.R.A. So many lives lost unnecessarily. It was all so futile. Now there was Ukraine and Gaza. What went on in the minds of these people who started wars and why didn't God strike them down before they could commit their evil deeds? It was all beyond her comprehension.

The service closed with The Lord's Prayer and everyone headed home. She walked alone back to her car parked by the church. A feeling of melancholy hung over her. There wasn't chance for a proper chat with Steve he was busy in his professional role. She'd have to wait until next time.

CHAPTER 34

Alexa Barber and Helena Hetherington, mum and sister of Erica Barber had arranged her baby shower in the function room of The Seven Stars pub in Mill Lane, Willows Dip. After the awful emotional turmoil she'd had throughout her pregnancy they wanted to make it a really special occasion for her, something to just focus on her and the baby instead of Harvey's shunning of them both. They wanted her to feel loved and cherished by her family and friends. They'd invited her work mates including Gemma who they were aware of being close to Harvey but they knew was also a good friend to Erica and it would have looked odd to have left her out.

Erica, looking blooming in a pale blue dress which showed off her growing bump, was delighted when they escorted her into the room adorned with blue and white balloons, bunting and tablecloths. They'd decided on afternoon tea and the sandwich choices had been pre-ordered so it didn't take long for their food and pots of tea and coffee to arrive. Along with the delicate floral china tea cups, saucers and plates, each place setting had a small gift bag with blue baby footprints on it, which contained games cards and party favours.

All talk was of babies and children as all the ladies were either mums, nanas, or aunties, and birth experiences were gleefully shared, not wishing to frighten the wits out of the Mum-to-Be! After the food was consumed the games commenced with the cards from the bags: guess the baby's weight, name suggestions etc. Another card had ten questions in emoji form depicting baby lifestyle and lots of laughs ensued at everyone's guesses. There were prizes for the winners. Then came the gift opening for the baby. Lots of cute outfits for him, toys, teddies, books, practical items such as bibs and vests, and Harvey's mum had crocheted an exquisite blue blanket for her first grandchild that was so intricate it brought tears to Erica's eyes.

"It's so beautiful. Thank you so much," she said giving her a hug. "It must have taken you ages."

"It kept me good while I was watching TV," she replied. "It's been years since I've crocheted; I didn't know if I'd remember how to do it so I had a look on YouTube and gave myself a refresher course. It all came back once I got going. I'm pleased with how it's turned out and I hope it keeps him warm."

"Oh it will, I'll use it all the time. It even matches the cake," Erica said, indicating it sitting in splendour on a side table waiting to be cut and eaten with replenished pots of tea and coffee. She'd take any remaining home to share with Harvey, make him feel a little bit a part of the day to see if it might instigate a thaw, she would always try anything. It depicted a baby covered in a blue blanket, expertly crafted, and she'd taken a photo to save to show him.

The whole afternoon had been thoroughly enjoyable and Erica felt lighter than she'd felt throughout her pregnancy. As they were packing the presents away Gemma took her aside for a moment.

"I just had to speak to you, I've been wanting to say it for ages but never got the chance. I overheard two of the girls at work talking in the stockroom one day saying you thought there was something between Harvey and me. They thought what a bitch I was with you pregnant and that I should stay away from him. I promise you Erica there's nothing between us and I'm sorry if you got that impression."

Erica felt her heartbeat quicken at the conversation for what else might be said. "I have worried about it yes. He's seemed much closer to you while he's pushed me away, and I'll be honest I've gone through agonies imagining the two of you together."

"No don't. I swear to you there's nothing like that. Harvey's a good friend but that's all there is to it. He's confided in me, he's very scared, overwhelmed by it all. I'm sure his feelings for you are still there, he talks about you a lot but it all happened before he'd even had time to think about whether he was ready for commitment. I think he'll be OK, just give him time. I know it must be difficult for you, but perhaps once the baby's born and he's got some hands on involvement, he'll find it's not as daunting as he expected."

"I hope you're right, and thanks for telling me this, it eases the worry a little."

It did. Erica found herself feeling more positive and uplifted by this whole afternoon than she'd felt all along. Perhaps everything would work out in the end.

Meanwhile Harvey found himself in St Luke's church. He didn't know why. He'd never been a big church-goer, Sunday school for a while as a child but that had soon tailed off when his mother was finding she had to drag him sulking and unwilling every Sunday. In the end she'd given in and they'd just stuck with his bedtime prayer. Now, here he was in his time of need.

He sat in the front pew of the empty church just staring at the altar, seeing yet not registering the cross in the centre flanked by the unlit candles in their holders, the gold cloth, the stained glass windows above it with the sun's rays illuminating, casting the colours of red, green, blue and yellow onto altar and floor. His thoughts went to the women at the baby shower, a female event enjoyed by his mother and his girlfriend, the mother of his unborn child.

What kind of father was he going to be if he couldn't love anymore? *Why* couldn't he love anymore? He'd loved Erica so much. They'd had such fun together, such a good relationship. He'd fancied her at work and couldn't believe his luck when she agreed to go out with him. He felt sure they'd have stayed together, moved in together, so why was he feeling this reluctance, this cooling off? It was as though he was emotionally dead. Even with his family who he knew he loved he still had to question it. Nothing seemed right and he didn't know what to do. He didn't know why he was in here or what he wanted to ask God.

"Are you OK there?" asked a voice at his side and he turned and looked up at the vicar standing in the aisle beside the pew, not in robes, just the dog collar denoting his status. He smiled a weak smile and nodded, then shook his head, not trusting himself to speak.

"Anything I can help with?" asked Steve noticing the tears form in the young man's eyes.

Harvey brushed them away with the back of his hand. "I don't know. I don't think anyone can."

Steve sat down beside him. "Try me."

Harvey looked down at his hands and the whole story flooded out on a torrent of words, about how unexpected it all was, how good things had been before, how inadequate he felt for Erica and his child, and how dead inside. "I just don't know what to do Vicar, and I don't know who to turn to. What kind of father and partner will I be if I can't face up to it?"

Steve realized who he was as soon as he mentioned Erica's name and he was glad he'd found him sitting here.

"Quite often thinking and worrying about a situation is a lot worse than when it actually happens. Have you spoken to anyone about it, shared your worries and your feelings?"

"A little. There's someone at work I talk to but she can't help, no-one can, no-one can change it, make it all go away, and I don't want anything to happen to the baby and I don't want to be without Erica, I just want us to be how we were before but we can never go back to that."

"Well if you don't want to be without her that says that your bond is still strong and you can build on that. Don't put pressure on yourself by trying to analyse why you feel the way you do, just take it a day at a time. If the only way you can be there for her at the moment is practically then go with that. It's a big change that's happened to you before you were ready and you need time to adjust. You'll probably find that once the baby arrives you'll be so busy taking care of his or her needs that you won't have time to think about how you feel. You'll pull together as parents and that will strengthen the bond that is still there."

"You can't be sure of that."

"No, we can't be sure of anything but I know how much of your life babies take up and believe me suddenly you come way down the list yourself. You've taken the first step by coming in here and talking it out with a stranger – me – now shall we talk it out with God?"

Harvey nodded.

They bowed their heads and Steve asked for God's guidance for this young man as he stepped into fatherhood, for the strength to support his family and the emotional peace in his new role. With the 'Amen' Harvey felt a sense of wellbeing he hadn't felt in a long time. It hadn't made everything right like waving a magic wand but it had soothed his tormented soul. He couldn't go home and tell Erica how much he loved her but he felt a warmth towards her return. It was a start.

He stood up to leave and clasped Steve's hand. "Thank you Reverend, you don't know what a help you've been to me."

"No problem. Anytime you need me I'm here."

Harvey and Erica arrived back at the same time and he helped her,

Helena and Alexa bring in presents, balloons and cake from Alexa's car. The girls were always pleasant and polite around him, treating him as some kind of ornament that might shatter if handled too harshly or on the other hand an explosive that might go off at any time. He felt bad about this as they'd all got on well together previously, been relaxed in each other's company and laughed a lot. Would this strain ever ease? Helena and Alexa didn't stay but headed home leaving the two of them together. Erica began unpacking gift bags.

"Look at all the lovely presents everyone has brought," she enthused. "People are so kind. We've got some cake left as well that we can have in a minute. I'll show you the photos of what it was like before we cut it."

"Looks like you had a good time," Harvey replied picking up a little dungaree suit with a giraffe on it. "This is cute isn't it."

"Yes, lovely, it's from Gemma." She wondered whether to mention their conversation but thought probably better not to. He seemed to be showing an interest which was more than he'd ever done before and she didn't want to spoil it. "Oh look what your mum made."

She picked up the parcel loosely covered in its wrapping to keep it clean and took out the blanket. "Isn't it absolutely gorgeous!"

He took it from her and opened it out. "Very clever Mum! I remember her knitting me some lovely jumpers when I was little, she used to be very good at crafts but she hasn't done as much as I've got older, I suppose she hasn't had the time with working. I'll text her later to say thank you."

Together they took out all the gifts and spread them on the kitchen table where Erica took photos. Harvey inspected several items, picking up toys, flipping through books.

"He's got the beginning of his library hasn't he." Erica commented.

"Certainly has! Quite a collection."

They stood the closest that they had in many weeks and Erica felt a subtle change in him. She wanted to reach out and touch him but didn't dare for spoiling the slight thaw. For Harvey, seeing the baby items laid out before him made it all seem a little less frightening. He could feel Erica's warmth beside him but he couldn't bring himself to touch her pregnant body. He didn't know why but the vicar had said don't try to analyse your feelings just go with it so he would for now. Today had been a good day for them both. Leave it at that.

CHAPTER 35

"Josh come quick," Jade called peeping through the blinds in their bedroom window, the dark of the winter night obscuring her from view from the lane.

He hurried in at the urgency of her tone. "You've not gone into labour have you?"

She laughed. "No not yet but look, it's all kicking off across the road. The police have arrived."

Sure enough P.C Jack Adams and P.C Lacey Miller were getting out of the police car and walking up to the house.

"They're having another soirée," Jade said, "I've been watching them arrive. Pull up a chair, bring the popcorn. Let the show begin."

As they watched the police entered the house.

"Ooh I'd love to be a fly on the wall," said Jade.

Josh laughed at her nosiness. "You're so funny how you watch their antics. You're a right Peeping Tom."

"It just fascinates me what they get up to. You hear about all manner of kinky stuff at these swinger's parties don't you. I'd never fancy it myself but I'd just like to know. I wonder if they have a playroom like in Fifty Shades?"

"You're such a naughty girl but I like it! Might have to think about a playroom ourselves."

"Might be difficult to explain to all these children you want me to have."

"Yes I suppose so. We'll just have to keep it to our fantasies."

"I wonder what sights have met the eyes of those two police officers? What states of undress people are in? They won't have to be easily embarrassed will they."

"I should imagine they've seen a lot worse in the line of duty than a bit of nakedness."

"I suppose so yeah. Oh look! They're bringing the shifty looking man out. I wonder what he's done? I bet he's the supplier, bringing the 'goods' for the pipes."

"He might have got a bit rough with somebody."

"I bet Vicki likes a bit of rough. She looks the type that's game for anything."

"Maybe he was more than she bargained for."

The handcuffed man was escorted to the police car and P.C Miller drove it away.

"I wonder if we'll ever find out what's gone on?" mused Jade.

"I'll see what I can gather through work but it may well be on social media."

Josh was a photographer for The Chronicle, the local paper so he was usually in the know about the gossip.

All went quiet then. No action from the lighted windows for the young couple's entertainment. The shifty one's arrest seemed to have put a dampener on proceedings.

A couple of days later Jade was in the post office, more for a nosey than a transaction and she scrutinized Vicki's features. There was a bruise around her eye, yellowing now and well disguised with make up, and a cut on her lip that was a few days old. Looked like the shifty one was a bit handy with his fists but she was speculating. Perhaps he'd bitten her, knocked her against a metal headboard? She told Josh when he got home and he also had news from work. A man, Daniel Jessop, had been arrested at a swinger's party accused of assault, released on bail.

CHAPTER 36

The first Sunday in December saw significant snowfall but the stalwart members of the congregation made it through. The churchyard path had been cleared and gritted but snow still fell giving a festive feel to the month of the Lord's birth.

Reverend Steve greeted his parishioners at the church door and was pleased to see Lavinia had braved the weather. He was always cheered that the look on her face mirrored what was surely on his own when they greeted each other but he still refused to acknowledge his feelings any further. Too dangerous to go there. It was enough to enjoy her company, for now at least.

The Simcock sisters arrived, crosspatch Lydia chiding downtrodden Sadie for wearing fashion boots with a heel and slithering all over the snow.

"You should have bought sensible boots at your age, something with a good grip to stop you falling, you could break something then I'd have to look after you. You're pushing sixty not twenty for goodness sake!"

"What and look like an old frump like you?" Sadie bit back.

Unusual for her Steve noticed, she mostly took what her sister said but he supposed she must get sick of it at times.

"I'd rather wear sensible boots and not slip than teeter about on those things you've got. There won't be any men in here looking at your legs in kinky boots."

"They're not kinky they're normal knee high boots with a heel but I suppose that's too fashionable for you." She cast a scathing look at her sister's clodhoppers. "I wouldn't be seen dead in them!"

"Well don't come crying to me when you break your leg."

"I won't. I'm more surefooted than you. Morning Vicar," she said turning her man-winning smile on Steve.

"Morning Sadie, Lydia. Glad you've wrapped up warmly against the weather. Good to see you."

They entered the church, stamping snow off their boots and made their way to their regular pew at the front.

Lavinia always sat at the back. She liked to be unobtrusive, didn't want people watching her watching Steve in case naked adoration was emblazoned across her face like a Michelangelo painting for all to see. Her staff at the florist were well aware of it and she felt like an adolescent fool to be hankering round after him when he'd shown her nothing more than friendship.

She told herself she wasn't attending church only to feel his hand upon her head when he blessed her, to share those eye locking moments throughout the service – did other people notice them she wondered? She told herself she felt an inner peace from the atmosphere, not quite found God as Jess said but a new awareness.

'A new awareness for whom?' her inner voice asked. 'Would you feel so drawn to the church if Lurch the Rector were leading the services? No, I think not.'

The first hymn was a carol as it was the beginning of Advent, The First Noel, and she and Steve exchanged a smile as they sang which filled her with a glow enough to melt the snow outside.

At the end of the service she stayed for coffee as she always did to get a few words with him before she left, her highlight of the day those brief moments alone, well, as alone as they ever got with his legion of followers. She sometimes felt he was Jesus Himself with his adoring crowds. Nobody had a bad word for him. She could see why and he was up there on a pedestal for her. With every day that dawned she loved him more. Yes she knew she loved him. It had to be acknowledged, she could deny it no longer. She'd been off men for so many years and now she had to go and fall for a vicar of all people! Surely he wouldn't be like other men, like the lying slimeball she'd been married too – would he? He'd only ever been pleasant towards her and he was just a man underneath the vestment, the same as any other man. They let you down one way or another and he couldn't know he was hurting her already by not responding in the way she wished.

"Have you driven here Lavinia or walked?" he was saying as he appeared beside her, and she felt her cheeks flush as she looked into his warm brown eyes, hoping he couldn't read her thoughts.

"I walked, I didn't think I'd chance it with the car because you can't tell how bad it's going to get can you. I've got sensible boots on." She pointed down and he smiled thinking of the Simcock sisters earlier conversation.

"Sensible and fashionable all at once."

"I hope so. Don't want to slip though. Still, quite a few turned out didn't they."

"Yes, more than I expected. Some people love snow, some hate it don't they. Which are you?"

"A bit in the middle. I've never liked driving in it. I don't mind a bit as long as we can all get about, it's gridlock I hate and when it keeps putting in an appearance in February and March when we're looking forward to a bit of spring warmth. What about you?"

"I can take it or leave it. It's weather isn't it, can't do anything about it."

An elderly couple came up to join them and Steve turned to speak to them so Lavinia said her goodbyes. It would take her a good fifteen minutes to walk home. As she stepped outside the snow was still falling, soft gentle flakes catching in her eyelashes and she thought of the face that had become so dear to her. If he didn't kiss her soon she'd explode.

CHAPTER 37

The village hall was abuzz with festivity for the Christmas fayre. The villagers were all out to purchase Christmas gifts for their loved ones and those with their own craft skills rented tables to sell their wares.

Connie Watson was a talented artist and she painted beautiful pictures of the birds at her sanctuary, various sizes to suit all budgets and home décor. She also made paint by numbers kits for children and adults alike who wanted to have a go at painting birds and wildlife, which she sold at the sanctuary towards its upkeep and at craft fayres.

Nathaniel O'Keefe did the same with his furniture business, crafting beautiful pieces of furniture to customers specifications: chairs, tables, cabinets, all exquisitely carved and polished. With the offcuts of wood he made small animals and birds. Passionate about wildlife he had hedgehogs, badgers, foxes, rabbits. He didn't paint them but polished them, preferring the natural look of the wood. He also sold them in Connie's souvenir shop at Little Acorn Bird Sanctuary and it benefitted them both.

Several tables along one wall were reserved for local authors, the two most successful and well known being Celia Wainwright and Tess Barker. Both made a comfortable living from their work; both were thankful that they'd had that element of luck in their books being in the right place at the right time to be seen by the right eyes to propel them into the spotlight. Other local authors, equally talented, had tables but hadn't had the luck to get onto book shop and supermarket shelves as Tess and Celia had but still got pleasure from their work. Bookworm Ella Hetherington, Adam's teenage daughter who worked in PageTurners book shop was drawn to these tables like a bee to a lavender field and a good proportion of her wages would be spent on them; she'd go home with armfuls of books. An avid reader, they'd keep her entertained throughout the Christmas period. For the authors it was an opportunity to promote their books.

One of the village ladies made spectacular greetings cards, and pieces of jewellery: earrings and keyrings, depicting guardian angels made of delicate beads, which she sold in aid of cancer research.

The Simcock sisters made the cakes and manned that stall – well Lydia made them, Sadie as usual was the stooge, albeit a dressed to kill stooge. People would say she did look good for almost sixty. Her reputation as a maneater went before her and it was a case of lock up your husbands. She didn't seem interested in a man long term, it was more the challenge for her. The women of the village didn't like to think of what went on once the poor innocent men had been lured into her web by lust. Whether men thought about it and had wild erotic fantasies nobody was telling. Perhaps Sadie needed it as a confidence booster from all of her sister's put downs. Perhaps her sister was jealous of Sadie's capabilities of snaring men. Who knew?

Their cake stall always looked delicious nevertheless and was very popular from the mince pies, Christmas cake slices, fairy cakes, to scones and biscuits. They brought a good supply and everything sold out. Not much sniping went on, apart from the odd, 'Be careful with that Sadie,' it was far too busy, Lydia had her work cut out enough serving customers to be observing Sadie's shortcomings. Likewise Sadie was too busy to be cruising the hall for men, well almost. She did like a little wander at some point. Nathaniel O'Keefe and Ellis Watson were always worth an exchange of words even though there was no chance of luring them away from their wives even briefly. Then there was Billy Marshall and Theo Stanyer, both hot but unattainable. A little light flirtation was very uplifting though especially away from her sister's sharp tongue. Then there was the handsome vicar. Oh yes, Willows Dip had its share of good looking men even if she couldn't get her sweaty mitts on them all.

Lavinia and her florist Jess had a stall this year selling Christmas wreaths and small arrangements. Jess also did her own sideline in framed, pressed flowers, very beautiful, especially those bright single flowers on a black background in a silver or gold frame. All stall holders operated their businesses online as well and had contact cards displayed on their tables to give out to interested viewers.

No Christmas fayre would be complete without Father Christmas and he was tucked away in his grotto at the back of the hall near the refreshment area for the children to visit.

Reverend Steve mingled among the tables and villagers chatting to everyone, pleased that it was well attended. Funds were always needed for the church roof! As he passed Lavinia's stall he gave her a smile and a wink, which didn't go unnoticed by Jess. She gave her own knowing smile to her friend.

"Nothing gets past you does it," grinned Lavinia.

"Not in affairs of the heart," replied Jess.

"I might just go and get a coffee. Do you want one?"

"Go on then but you can't fool me, you're going on the hunt for the slick vic, I know your game. Off you go, I'll hold the fort."

Lavinia's grin got wider as she almost skipped off and a lady asked Jess about the framed, pressed flower. It was a yellow rose on a black background.

"This is beautiful. I've always wanted to be able to press flowers but never been successful. I've got some red roses from my husband for our ruby wedding and I'd love to save one. Could you do it for me please?"

"Are they still fresh?"

"Yes, it was only yesterday."

"Bring one into the shop to me tomorrow and I'll do it for you."

"Oh would you! That would be fabulous! Thank you so much."

Meanwhile Lavinia had managed to catch up with Steve by the refreshments hatch at the kitchen.

"It seems to be going well doesn't it," she said to him.

"It does," he answered picking up his cup. "I always love this event, such a good buzz about it. How's your stall doing?"

"Good thanks, sold a few arrangements and a couple of wreaths."

"I guess you do well on them at Christmas."

"We do yes. Busy time."

They were standing so close their hands were almost touching. He smelled divine. Divine was a good adjective for a man of God, but she felt it more of the senses. That hint of aftershave, plus just him, the essence of him, the cleanliness of him.

"Ooh more tea Vicar," chimed in Sadie Simcock sashaying past and breaking into any closer proximity that might develop and Lavinia felt herself bristle. If she had any mystical powers she'd have twisted the woman's ankle to get her out of the way. Then again perhaps not. It might have twisted the wrong way and knocked her straight into Steve's arms and that would have banjaxed the whole plan. Best leave the magical powers to those best suited to them.

"Always time for more tea Sadie," replied Steve jovially.

Somebody else barged in between them and Lavinia gave a silent sigh. 'Give up,' said her inner voice. 'Just get the coffees and go.' Disappointment and anger battled within her core and pragmatism ousted them both.

"Did you manage a chat?" asked Jess when she returned.

"Barely," scowled Lavinia. "Always somebody butting in."

"I suppose that goes with his job."

"Yeah suppose."

Later as they were leaving and putting the unsold items in the boot of Lavinia's car she confided in Jess.

"I don't know whether I'm coming or going with all this. Of all the damn fool things to do, why do I have to go and fall for a vicar!"

"It's not as if we can choose is it. It just happens. It's not something you can switch on and off."

"No it isn't. I didn't need this. I was quite happy going along with my flowers. I had no intention of looking at a man again, ever, and then all of this comes along. It messes with your head Jess and I could do without it."

"I know. I don't envy you. I'm glad me and Matt are settled with the kids, I wouldn't want to have to go through it all again. The, does he like me, doesn't he like me, am I imagining it all?"

"I know, and the overthinking! Do you think men do it?"

Jess shrugged. "Who knows? It's the girls are from Venus, men are from Mars thing isn't it."

Just then Steve came out and walked past them, trailing an arm across Lavinia's shoulder and giving it a squeeze. Her heart almost leapt out of her chest.

"Goodnight ladies," he said as he walked on. "Did you have a productive one?"

"Yes thanks," Jess replied, Lavinia could barely speak.

"Do you think he heard us?" she gasped to Jess when he was out of earshot.

"Nah, shouldn't think so."

"He touched me! We've had contact! Well we have when he blesses me but that's work isn't it; this was different."

"There you are. You can go to bed a happy woman tonight. Sweet dreams."

CHAPTER 38

Christmas was always a busy time in the church calendar, lots of special services and Steve found himself extra busy. Of all the services two of his favourites had to be carol singing by candlelight with the church bathed in the soft glow of the flickering light, and the crib service for the children. The wonder on their young faces as they looked in at the baby Jesus in the manger surrounded by ox and ass, shepherds with their sheep, Mary and Joseph, the angel up above, never failed to move him yet it was tinged with a hint of cynicism as to how many would continue to believe as they grew into teens and adults.

His own two sons, twins, David and Mark, identical but for a small mole behind Mark's ear, now in their twenties, hadn't followed in his footsteps and gone into the church. Both had questioned it as they'd hit their teens and while not atheist they found it a bit of a fairy story, which saddened him. However you couldn't force your beliefs on your children, you taught them when they were young then left them to make their own minds up. Lisa, his ex, their mother, had the belief though not as strongly as him but she'd never forced her opinions on them either. Nevertheless he always hoped that the majority of the children who gazed in wonder at the crib scene would maintain some form of belief however small.

It was true that numbers in congregations were decreasing and were predominantly older people. Possibly young families were too busy with work commitments with both parents having careers. In his younger days a good percentage of mothers stayed at home with under fives then had part time jobs so perhaps had more time. He didn't like to think it was a lack of belief in God but he supposed that had to be a factor. Everyone would have their own experiences therefore their own faith and for his own part all he could do was to make his church and parish as welcoming as possible with many activities available to all ages in the village hall. From birth there was the breastfeeding group, baby massage, toddler group, play group, and for adults, book club, knit and natter and coffee mornings. It was a good community atmosphere and some young families did attend church and bring their children to Sunday school but he'd have liked more.

On a more personal level he found his thoughts turning increasingly to Lavinia and her presence in church and in his life. She was a lovely woman, very warm and friendly and he was drawn to her in a way he couldn't explain. He'd just had to touch her as they were leaving the Christmas fayre the other night. It hadn't been planned, a conscious thought when he'd squeezed her shoulder, it had just happened. He'd wanted to hug her, hold her, cuddle her as you would anyone you were fond of but it was more than that with her and he wouldn't tread that path. They'd had their earlier chat interrupted by Sadie Simcock, then others had come between them to get refreshments and when he'd turned back she'd gone.

He didn't know where all this had come from. He didn't want

a relationship but he did feel he wanted her company. That would be moving into different territory though. He couldn't have her company without a relationship and all that it entailed, sleeping together, making love. No, he couldn't allow himself to go there. He hadn't even allowed himself to think about kissing her because once he crossed that line into the realms of fantasy he'd have to follow it through and it was such a massive step. He'd been single for far too long, it would be like a teenager starting all over again but with the life experience of failure. Inwardly he was torn in two. Half of him wanted her in every possible way, body and soul, the other half wanted to run from her shouting, 'Nooo,' in case it should all go wrong again. What to do about this emotional turmoil? He hoped that God would be his guide.

CHAPTER 39

Christmas was a time for family and in this Steve was no different to anyone else. After his morning service he was going over to Mark and his partner Lucy for Christmas Dinner. David and his partner Grace would be joining them then the young people would go over to Lisa and her husband for a buffet tea in the evening and Steve would return home alone to relax after the hectic activity of the month. He'd enjoy putting his feet up with a glass of whisky and a few chocolates.

Mark greeted him at the door of his and Lucy's apartment. "Merry Christmas Dad. How's the God business?" he said giving him a hug and clapping him on the back.

"Very busy but the heat is off a bit now. Have you had a good morning?"

"Probably a bit more relaxing than yours."

They went through to the kitchen diner where Lucy was putting the finishing touches to the meal, which smelled delicious, roasting turkey, stuffing, all the vegetables, especially sprouts, Steve's favourite. David and Grace had already arrived and were seated at the table. It wasn't a large apartment so the atmosphere was rather cosy but they all squeezed in together as they sat down to eat. Mark and Lucy served directly onto plates with space on the table at a premium and no room for vegetable tureens, just space for jugs of bread sauce and gravy, both of which were refilled as needed.

Conversation was mainly centred on work. David and Grace were both in I.T and Steve had no idea what their jobs entailed. He only understood technology as far as he needed it for his own work, anything beyond that was lost on him so their comments went completely over his head; he just concentrated on his sprouts with their blanket of gravy.

Mark had followed Steve's father into joinery with a love of wood from a child and the pair had always had a close bond. He was working on a new housing estate and he and Lucy were saving for a deposit on one of the houses. Lucy was a teaching assistant at a primary school near to where they lived.

After Christmas pudding had been consumed everyone helped clear the table, Mark stacked the dishwasher and they all retired to the sofas for the present opening. The attractively wrapped parcels with sparkling bows and tags were collected from around the tree and handed out to each recipient and a lot of laughter ensued at the joke presents: socks with captions on the soles saying, 'do not disturb the vicar,' the bad joke book, the usuals of wine, beer and chocolates, then they all relaxed with their favourite tipple to chat comfortably and as the early winter twilight descended, lamps were lit adding their soft glow to that of the tree and garland lights and Christmas enveloped them in its embrace.

"Who's Lavinia?" Lucy asked Steve.

"She's just one of my parishioners."

"You mention her a lot. You sound quite fond of her."

"Yes I suppose I am."

Mark's eyes twinkled. "How fond?"

Steve grinned. "Fond enough."

"Ooh romantically?" asked Grace. "I love a bit of romance."

"Steady on," replied Steve, "I'm fond of lots of people."

"But not in *that* way?" queried David.

Steve winked. "I never said *that* way."

Mark said, "Come on Dad spill, do you fancy the lovely Lavinia?"

Steve laughed. "I don't know about fancy."

"But you like her."

"Yes."

A collective cheer went up.

"Are you going to ask her out?" David said.

"Good heavens no!"

"Why not?"

"I haven't even thought about it."

"Well perhaps you should," Lucy added, "think about it I mean."

"Does she like you?" Grace asked.

"I suppose so," Steve replied.

"Romantically?"

"I don't know."

"You could test the water."

"How would I do that? Erm, hang on a minute! Who are you lot? My dating agency?"

"We'd just like to see you happy," said Mark.

"I am happy."

"No but with a bit of company."

"I don't know. It's a big step. I've been single a long time, set in my ways. I don't know if I want to give that up. It has crossed my mind but if it all kicked off it would be a massive change and I don't know if I'd want that and I most certainly couldn't go through another divorce. No, best just leave things as they are."

David looked across at his brother. "Well I think we should go along to the next church event don't you bro, get a look at the little lady."

Steve looked horrified. "You hadn't better! Anyway there's nothing you'd be interested in."

"We could come for Palm Sunday," said Mark. "I always liked that when we had the procession with the palm crosses."

"No need to get yourselves back on the religious roundabout much as I'd like to encourage a young congregation."

"Oh I don't know," Grace added, "it sounds like fun and a bit of matchmaking thrown in."

"Don't you dare! Anyway haven't you got another party to go to and I'm ready to go home and put my feet up. Thanks for a lovely dinner and a fabulous day and all the presents."

"You're welcome," Mark said, "thanks for yours too. "We'll have to come and pay you a visit soon."

"That'll be great, just not in church!"

Later as he sat at home with his whisky and chocolates Steve pondered on the conversation with his young people. Did he want them to meet Lavinia? Her to meet them? He would like that but could he trust his family to be discreet? He wouldn't want any suggestions making that he wouldn't feel comfortable with or feel he had to follow through. It was a while until Easter and he couldn't see them putting in an appearance at a regular Sunday service. He'd think the matter over and talk it through with them first. He didn't want them going along and putting their great size tens in it!

CHAPTER 40

Lavinia's Christmas followed a similar theme but she'd gone to her brother John and his wife Jayne and their twelve and ten year old sons Tom and Mike. The boys were at that in between age where she was never sure what to give them as presents. They were into their PlayStations so a gift card was useful but not like a present to open. She hoped she got the clothes right with whatever named brand they were wearing, and something connected to football went down well but it was a challenge not to be too predictable. Chocolate gifts were acceptable too.

After a delicious Christmas Dinner when everyone was too full to move and the presents had been exchanged, the boys vanished to their rooms to their PlayStations to do whatever they did with the cards and the three adults sat on the sofas with a glass of wine.

"So how's your vicar?" asked Jayne.

Lavinia sighed wistfully. "Oh that he were my vicar." She looked down into her glass as if seeing his face in the ruby red liquid. "All we ever do is chat and keep getting interrupted by one of his flock."

"I'm surprised you're interested in anyone after being single all this time."

"No more surprised than me and I have to go and fall for a vicar!"

"Perhaps that's why you fell for a vicar," reasoned John. "Maybe subconsciously you felt he'd be a more decent character, less likely to hurt you."

"Maybe. It's all very weird. It just kind of crept up on me but the more you try to get someone out of your mind the more they seem to keep sneaking back in."

"It is a difficult one isn't it," Jayne added. "It's not like you could behave like you could with any other sort of man, lay your cards on the table as it were."

"Ha, I'd never dare do that anyway, fear of rejection. I've always been backward in coming forward. It's not easy with a vicar though. I've wondered if I'm being too obvious, being at every church event, harvest supper, Christmas fayre, all the services, but I can't stay away, I just have to be where he is. All of my friends know."

"Do you think he does?"

"I don't know. If he does either he's not interested or he's not doing anything for a reason. I get sick of thinking about it. He's just a man isn't he and they do your head in."

"It would be nice to see you settle with somebody," John said. "I've never liked the thought of you being on your own although you seem happy enough. I think everybody needs company."

"I suppose we do. I don't really think about it. I am happy on my own; I'm content with my own company. I like doing what I want when I want, not bothering if I don't want to. All that would have to change if I was with someone but I suppose life, the universe, whatever it is, has its plan and what's meant will be."

"Yes I suppose that's one way of looking at it."

Lavinia finished her wine then stood up. "Well I'll get back now and get my pjs on to watch Call the Midwife. Thanks for a lovely day and the presents. I'll just shout up good night to the boys but they probably won't hear me."

Once she was seated in front of the TV with more wine and chocolates, comfortable in her best pyjamas, a little more glamorous than her usual fleecy ones, waiting for the programme to start, her thoughts as ever turned to Steve. What was he doing? The same as her? She knew he'd been invited to one of his twin sons for dinner. Was he home now and watching TV? How wonderful it would be if they could text each other on WhatsApp and compare their days but they hadn't even exchanged numbers; he'd never asked her and she couldn't ask him. You didn't go asking the vicar for his number, even Sadie Simcock wouldn't do that. For the millionth time she wondered where on earth all of this was heading if anywhere. She didn't know what to do about it, didn't know what to think about it. All she could do was keep going with it a day at a time. She couldn't put him out of her mind, she'd tried. She'd thought should she stay away from him? Would that help? Perhaps it ought to be her New Year's resolution. If there was no positive progression by then she should stop going to church. What if she saw him in the street though and he asked her why she'd stopped going? She could hardly say it's because I'm in love with you and you're not in love with me could she! Oh why had God or the universe or whoever the hell it was put her in this position and not just left her alone to get on with her life with her flowers?

CHAPTER 41

New Year's Eve was party time in Willows Dip as the villagers celebrated with the rest of the world. The lights on the tree outside the shops opposite St Luke's church shone brightly, twinkling in the chill night air. The Seven Stars pub in Mill Lane was doing a roaring trade and it was a ticket only night for the buffet. As midnight struck, counted down on the screen with Big Ben, the pub erupted with 'Happy New Year,' followed by Auld Lang Syne. Fireworks went off in the neighbouring gardens as 2024 was rung in.

Fireworks of a different kind altogether had ignited in Jade and Josh's cottage as Marnie Elise had decided to put in an appearance at last after making them wait an extra week.

"Mum you'll have to put the cork back in the champagne," Jade rang and told Donna at tea time. "Party plans will have to go on hold, we're off to the hospital. Contractions are every five minutes.

Meet you there."

"OK darling I'm on my way. It was only Theo and I with cheese and biscuits and a few drinks anyway. He won't mind settling down with a film."

By the time Donna arrived Jade was already on the gas and air and labour was being monitored.

"You're doing great," encouraged Josh, wincing with the strength of her grip on his hand. "Keep going."

"I bloody am!" she gasped. "And you're never coming near me again! You can forget the barefoot and pregnant!"

Donna stood back to let them have their time together, there as moral support for her daughter and if Josh needed a toilet break. She remembered her own labour with Jade and had had pretty much the same sentiment. It was a pain you forgot though albeit she and Ellis hadn't had other children. It was hard to watch her daughter in that pain now and be unable to do anything about it but it was a woman's role in life, God willing, and Josh was very supportive of her, holding her hand, smoothing the hair back from clinging to her damp forehead with her efforts, offering her sips of water.

The hours ticked on and with one final push Marnie Elise made her entrance into the world at twenty five past midnight on the 1st of January 2024.

"The first 2024 baby!" exclaimed the midwife. "Let's take her and weigh her."

She whisked her away and did her checks. "7lbs 12oz, very healthy." She passed her to Jade for skin to skin contact, then next to Josh.

Donna now had a role as photographer, capturing the first moments of the new family. Jade pink cheeked, exhausted but happy smiled down at her daughter, up at Josh, across at her mother.

"Send Dad the pictures," she said to her.

"I will, don't worry."

"Tell him he can come and see her later today. I can't wait to show him. His first grandchild."

"It's very exciting," replied Donna. "I can't believe I'm a nana."

After the skin contact the baby was wrapped up and a cotton hat put on and the new nana had her first hold of her granddaughter. She marvelled at the exquisite perfection of the tiny features, the rosebud mouth, eyes just open and taking the first look at her world. She then handed her to Jade for the first try at breastfeeding.

"It'll never go in her tiny mouth," she wailed.

"It will," the nurse encouraged, "you'll get the knack of getting her to latch on. She won't take much now she'll be tired from the birth, it's only to get you both started, pick up on her sucking reflex."

"Eeow it hurts!"

"We'll get you some cream."

After the attempt had been made a nurse took the baby to be bathed and put her in her cot to sleep and left Jade to rest. Josh and Donna both went home for some rest themselves.

Later that afternoon Ellis brought Olivia, Jade's nineteen year old half sister to see her and the baby.

"She's beautiful darlin'," he said kissing Jade's forehead, "just like her mum."

"Pick her up if you want to."

"I don't want to wake her. Besides, it's been a long time since I handled a baby."

"Go on Dad, I'm dying for a hold," said Olivia, so he lifted her out very gently.

"See she hasn't woken has she," Jade said. "Still sleeping off the meds."

"Have they said when you can go home?" he asked.

"Today, teatime when Josh comes back."

"Was it bad?" asked Olivia nervously.

Jade decided not to tell her about the stitches. "It was and it wasn't. It is painful but it's a kind of productive pain that you're doing something about and it stops when they're born, then you've got your baby!"

"Shall you have another?"

"Give us a chance! I haven't got over this yet. The thought of anything going on down there is a big no no."

"Let's have a hold then Dad," said Olivia.

Ellis transferred the baby to her auntie. "Make sure you support her head."

"How does it feel to be a granddad?" Jade asked.

Ellis laughed. "Old but good. I'm just relieved you're both OK. I spent a worrying night but Josh's texts were very helpful, kept us all in the loop. I was relieved to hear she'd arrived safely and all was well. Connie was too and sends her love. She'll see you as soon as you're ready."

"Yes I'm glad she's here safe and sound. Just need to settle in at home now. Connie's welcome anytime."

The next few days were hectic with visits from family and friends to see the new arrival. Especially keen to see her was three year old Noah, Jake and Helena's son, she'd be his first cousin. His sister Daisy at sixteen months old didn't understand about babies and had to be watched carefully around Marnie in case curiosity got the better of her and she got a bit heavy handed. Noah wanted to know if he could hold her.

"Sit on the sofa," said Josh and we'll put cushions around you. She'll be heavy for you."

Like the old hand that he was Noah added, "I know about babies, I've held Daisy."

Josh grinned at his nephew. "Of course you have. How could I forget."

As always Josh was ready with his camera. He'd enjoyed all the photos immensely. Throughout Jade's pregnancy he'd liked the natural shots and now he couldn't get enough of her breastfeeding.

"Just rein yourself in," she'd told him. "I'm not at the serene motherhood stage yet, it's bloody painful and Marnie and I are still learners."

"Pose for me then without actually feeding if that's more comfortable."

"OK but make them discreet, I don't want everything on show especially if you publish any."

"Well I had thought we could use some to promote breastfeeding or for mother and baby competitions. What do you think?"

"It would depend on the photo. I'd have to have the last say which one you used. I don't want the world and his wife looking at my naked breasts."

"They're very nice breasts," he said appreciatively.

"I'm glad you think so but I don't want the public to be too familiar with me, especially as my boobs will be fulfilling their purpose, I wouldn't dare walk down the street!"

"OK you can choose the image"

Back to the task in hand he focussed on Noah with Marnie and they managed to get Daisy to sit still for a few moments to get the three cousins in a few shots together for the family album, then Helena lifted the baby off her son so he could go and play.

"I always think babies are little miracles aren't they," she said looking into the tiny face. "How's she sleeping?" she asked turning to Jade who was trying to rest on the sofa whilst other people were there to hold the baby.

"The first night quite well, I think tired after the birth. The next couple not so good. We were awake every two hours with her, she seems a bit windy. You never know if you're doing right do you although we can always text someone and I've texted Mum a lot in the day. She's been great, she's called in to help every day. Josh is on the washing which there seems to be loads of when she's burping sick up."

"You'll soon settle into a routine. How long paternity leave have you got Josh?"

"Two weeks but I can be flexible with my hours after that."

Jake came over to take the baby from his wife to have a look at her. "Who do you think she's like?" he asked.

"The dark hair is from both sides of the family isn't it, Jade and her dad, Dad Nathaniel and his family, but then there's blonde from both our mums so she may go lighter. We'll have to see," Josh answered.

"I can see my dad a bit," commented Jade.

"Yes I can see him," Jake added looking into her face.

"They usually say the firstborn daughter is the female version of her father don't they," put in Helena."

"Yes, maybe there's a look of Josh about her too. Always interesting I think, family resemblances, you can often see different people can't you, sometimes expressions as they get older. We're all just a mish mash of genes aren't we."

"Yes marvellous isn't it really." Jade yawned. "Oh dear excuse me, I don't think I've ever been so tired. I've never known sleep depravation before."

"We'll go," said Helena. "We only wanted to call and see you and meet Marnie. I know how tiring it is, you need to rest while you can and establish a routine."

Jade went to get up to see them out.

"No, don't get up, stay where you're comfy and try to rest while the baby sleeps."

Jake handed her to Josh and she slept on. "I'll see if she'll settle in her pram for a while although she seems to like to be on us."

"Yeah ours did," his brother replied. "See if you can settle her, we'll see ourselves out. I hope you can get a bit of sleep."

CHAPTER 42

The next cousin to arrive for the Hetherington children Noah and Daisy was Auntie Erica and Uncle Harvey's baby, Isaac Harvey. They'd been informed of his arrival by their mother Helena, Erica's sister. He'd weighed in at 7lbs 2oz a day over his due date of 4th January, on the 5th at 1 a.m. Daisy was still too young to understand all these babies but Noah was very interested.

"When can we see him?" he'd asked excitedly.

"Once they've settled in at home. We'll go and visit and you can give him the blue teddy bear we've bought him."

Helena had been for a very short visit to the hospital to get a bit of sister time with Erica and see how the birth had gone.

"Let's say I've had better experiences. I'm not in any rush to repeat it, not that that's likely under the circumstances," Erica had responded, "and you never told me about the stitches!!"

Helena had laughed. "Well I'd thought it was best not to scare you with that, after all you might not have needed many."

"Wrong! I thought she was embroidering a blanket down there! I'd sooner have had another baby. I won't be able to sit for a week."

"How about the feeding?"

"That as well. He's going on the bottle. I don't do pain."

Helena dropped her voice to a whisper. "How was Harvey?"

"He'd never win birth partner of the year. He looked as though he'd rather be anywhere else than here. Paced up and down licking his lips, I thought he was either going to pass out or be sick. I said at one point it's me who's having this baby not you but he just looked even more uncomfortable so I just went back to sucking the gas and air and left him to his pacing."

"Mum was here though wasn't she. Did she help?"

"Oh yes. She had her work cut out trying to reassure us both, quite laughable really, I could feel for her now when I think about it, she seemed torn between the two of us, trying to involve Harvey who looked like he'd bolt from the room like a caged tiger if someone left the door open long enough, and me wailing make it go away," she tittered. "Poor Mum, she seemed at her wits end. I think she was as glad as I was when the baby arrived. She had something to do then taking photos, texting everyone, and of course getting to hold him."

"How was Harvey then?"

"Better. He held him and did the skin to skin and sat with him while Mum took photos to send to everyone including his parents who were waiting for news. There was no miraculous moment of wonderment but he did show some interest."

"How's he been since?"

"OK from a practical sense. Got everything I've needed, the nurse helped him dress the baby, he seemed to enjoy that and was quite pleased with himself, he's getting used to handling him so perhaps he'll be a help. Maybe he'll feel better now he's got an active role to play."

That had been yesterday and now Helena was waiting to hear from her sister to say when they could visit.

As with their visit to Jade and Josh, Noah and Daisy were positioned suitably for photos with their new cousin, along with the blue teddy bear gift. As children do they soon got bored. Daisy was at that age where she was investigating everything and if it wasn't fastened down she'd picked it up and carried her prize to show her anxious parents should she drop some precious memento – not that Harvey in his present state of distance had showered Erica with memorable gifts. Thus it was that the visit wasn't a long one and Jake and Helena having once introduced their offspring to their new cousin bundled them off home and left Erica and Harvey to begin some sort of routine.

He's due a feed," Erica said. "Shall I get it or you?"

"I'll get it. You get him ready."

She was happy to go along with that, adjusting her sitting position to as near to comfortable as she could get with the stitches whilst holding the baby. Harvey brought the bottle in and handed it to her.

"Just check the temperature, I think it's OK."

She did and nodded. "Yes it's fine, thanks."

It was still a bit new getting Isaac into position to feed but he settled to his bottle and Harvey sat next to them to watch him take it until he'd had enough, then Erica sat him up to burp him. Other actions also took place.

"Oh, looks like he's going to need changing."

Harvey leapt into action fetching changing mat and the box containing wipes, cream and nappies and Erica had to admit she couldn't fault him on the practical issues, he seemed quite hands on. He took the baby from her and laid him on the mat, removing his clothes.

"Oh nooo!" he wailed. "He's covered! It's all up his back, all that black stuff."

"Meconium." She eased herself off the sofa. "It'll be easier to bath him. Can you get the worst off?"

"Yes."

"I'll get the bath ready."

Between them the new parents bathed their tiny infant, unaware of the first tentative silken threads drawing them closer and beginning to stitch their severed bond. More stitches were added during the small hours of the night as Isaac woke for a feed. Harvey warmed the bottle then sat on the bed beside Erica as she fed him.

"He's not taking it properly," she said with a worried tone as Isaac kept twisting and crying. "He seems very windy, I can feel his tummy gurgling."

"Here let me have a try." He took the baby from her and repositioned him and eventually he settled and took the bottle. He burped him, Erica changed him but Isaac was quite awake and lay on the changing mat on the bed, quite contented, just looking round the room in the dim light from the bedside lamp.

Erica smiled. "He's getting to know his surroundings."

Harvey returned the smile. "Yes, I wonder what he's thinking? Wherever am I?" He looked at his son taking in every exquisite feature of the child's face. "He's so perfect isn't he."

"He is. We're very lucky to have him aren't we."

"We are."

After a while the baby's eyelids began to close and they settled him into his pod on the side of Erica's bed. After a moment's hesitation Harvey got into bed and Erica joined him. They lay close but not quite touching and didn't hold or kiss each other but it was enough for now.

CHAPTER 43

"The Lord is here."

"His spirit is with us,"

"Lift up your hearts."

"We lift them to the Lord."

The Epiphany service was underway and the villagers of Willows Dip were out for Sunday worship signalling the end of the Christmas period.

Jade and Josh had brought Marnie Elise along for her first blessing and having been fed, changed and made comfortable in her pram they hoped she'd sleep throughout the service and wouldn't be too disturbed to be got out for the blessing. Dressed in pink and white she'd been admired by a good many people on their way into church; they'd walked as it wasn't far and the fresh air would do them all good, plus it was another excuse to use the pram and take turns to push it, Jade and Josh had both basked in that golden glow of proud parents.

All went to plan and Jade lifted the baby out gently so as not to wake her as they went up to the altar for their blessings. For Reverend Steve he always felt an extra special something to give a first blessing to a baby, a kind of protection given on behalf of God, a privilege of his mission.

Today was extra special as far as blessings went. An Epiphany blessing was to be given out to every parishioner to bless their homes and all who inhabited them. This was in the form of a piece of chalk which was blessed by Reverend Steve and given to everyone along with a slip of paper bearing the blessing to be performed when they got home.

Lavinia was in church as always and the chalk was almost like a lover's gift to her. She knew it wasn't; she knew she was getting a little bit crazy but that's what love did to you, made you a little bit crazy. She and Steve hadn't got to the stage of exchanging gifts – indeed any stage at all – so this tiny piece of chalk took on massive proportions in her psyche. Her rational mind told her it wasn't anymore a special gift to her than it was to the rest of the congregation and she knew that but it was still from him, the first thing he'd given her – maybe the only thing he ever would – and she'd treasure it. The slip of paper that came with it read thus:

How to bless your home at Epiphany.
Use the blessed chalk to write:
20+C+M+B+24
Above or near the doorway.
2024 for the year
C, M, B, for the 3 Magi
Casper, Melchior, and Balthasar
And for
Christus Mansionem Benedicat
Latin for, 'May Christ bless this house.'
As you are writing pray this prayer.
Lord God of Heaven and Earth

You revealed your only begotten son

To every nation by the guidance of a star.

Bless this house and all who inhabit it.

Fill us with the light of Christ, that our concern for others may reflect your love.

We ask this through Christ our Lord.

Amen.

On reaching home she dropped her bag and keys on the table, removed her coat and sat down to read the slip of paper properly, she'd only scanned through it in church. She wouldn't do it straight away she'd have her lunch first then concentrate fully on it, give it all of her attention, do a proper job. She'd also done a proper job on lunch today and put a chicken in to roast with potatoes before she went out so the aroma that greeted her when she arrived home and opened the door was a delight to the senses and her hunger pangs increased. She'd even made an apple crumble which would only need reheating in the oven whilst she ate the roast. Delicious.

As she sat at the table alone but not lonely she couldn't help but think how lovely it would be if Steve could come back with her one day and share it. Would it ever happen or was it just a silly dream somewhere in her stupid mind intent on tormenting her? Nevertheless she enjoyed her meal, and the dessert, stacked and started the dishwasher then put her mind to the blessing.

As she climbed on the chair to write with the chalk above the door she hoped that God and Jesus would forgive her for thinking of the handsome vicar who was never out of her thoughts, reciting the words of the prayer.

CHAPTER 44

Josh was delighted with himself. His photograph of Jade and Marnie in repose in the nursery chair, Jade's aspired serene motherhood image, had won first prize in a mother and baby competition and he'd had another one used in a magazine to promote breastfeeding. He was showing them to his sister Liliana and her boyfriend of two years Ryan, who were frequent visitors. Lili loved the babies, Jake's two and now Marnie but she wasn't ready for her own yet she was concentrating on her career. She had a science degree and was working in the pathology laboratory at the hospital, which she loved but she was interested in genetics and hoped to move into that field in the future. Ryan was a postman with Royal Mail, had been for a number of years but wasn't happy. There had been a lot of controversy recently over their treatment of employees and he wanted out but he hadn't decided which way out.

"They're great photos Josh," Lili said. "You're very good Jade to let him photograph you in private moments."

Jade grinned. "He's always photographing me, he'd photograph me naked if I'd let him but you have to draw the line somewhere don't you." (She didn't mention their private collection of photos.) "I told him the breastfeeding photos would have to be discreet, I don't want to bump into people in the street knowing they've seen my naked breasts, or have them plastered on billboards for all to see!"

"He gets it from Mum and Dad, all the sex," Lili added. "They can't keep their hands off each other, at their age either! You'd think they'd have got fed up by now!"

"Do you think you ever get fed up of it?" asked Josh.

"Well the novelty must wear off when you know everything about each other don't you think?"

"Oh I don't know," Ryan winked at her, "you always seem pretty adventurous, perhaps you've got a bit of your mum and dad in you as well!"

She gave him a playful slap. "Hey you! Don't go giving away our secrets."

"Ho ho, little sis is a bit wild in the bedroom is she?" Josh teased.

"It has been known," Ryan twinkled.

"You're making me blush," said Lili coyly.

"Ha that'll be the day when you blush," Josh said, "I'm sure it's never been known."

"I might in Jade's position if you wanted to photograph my flesh."

"I'm just glad I'm his only model," said Jade. "I wouldn't mind his sultry sister with her wild Romany looks but I'd object to any other woman. I'm pleased that wildlife is his passion."

"Speaking of Mum and Dad I said I'd go over one day to see Izzy but I haven't had chance. Is she OK?"

Izzy was Josh's border collie who had stayed in her home with Chloe and Nathaniel when Josh had isolated with Jade at her mother Donna's home during the Covid 19 lockdown of 2020, then they'd subsequently bought the cottage they lived in now. Izzy had picked up a virus had been sick necessitating a vet's visit but seemed to be over the worst.

"She's fine," Lili told him. "Dad still enjoys walking her in the woods. I think it reminds him of his younger days when he lived there in the caravan with his dog Jet and the fox he took in, Tag. He has very fond memories of those two and those days, and when he and Mum met in those woods, even though she was married to Adam at the time and they had a lot of heartache to live through. It's a funny old world isn't it, relationship break ups, who ends up with whom."

"Yes," Jade added, "my parents are both happy with the people they're with now. I was only six when Dad met Connie and I must admit I wasn't always nice to her; I wanted him back with Mum, plus I didn't want to share him but they were happy and gave me a sister in Olivia and I love them all. Years later Mum met Theo and I never thought she'd want to be with anyone else, she's always been very driven by business, I think that's why she and Dad broke up, she had more time for the business than she did for him but it just works for her and Theo. Maybe because he's a businessman too even though he's restricted by long covid, they seem in tune somehow. Perhaps it's all to do with soul mates or perhaps some people don't meet the right person until later in life. All very strange isn't it."

"Yes, all planned by the universe, written in the stars. Anyway isn't it time my niece woke up so I can have a cuddle?"

CHAPTER 45

It was a rare, dry Sunday afternoon and the neighbours of Regent Grove were taking advantage of the brief respite in the relentless rain and having a January tidy up in their gardens.

Lavinia had been to church and had a chat to Steve which neither thrilled nor depressed her. Their friendship/potential relationship, whatever you wanted to call it had stagnated and she was steeling herself to accept that he was only interested in her as a friend. She'd almost given up on the longed for kiss – almost but not quite, something always came to mind to make her feel that hope was not lost, song lyrics, something someone said, a random throwaway comment about something totally unrelated but which held a meaning for her, but then she'd sigh and think oh just give up. She was out now hoping a bit of fresh air and the garden would fill her mind with something other than futile adolescent notions.

She looked over the road in the corner of the cul de sac to where

Donna and Theo were in the garden in coats and gardening gloves and had paused to chat to their friends Tess and Billy who were out for a stroll. Their next door neighbours Gervais and Gavin emerged from their front door with their two little Papillion dogs to take them for their walk. Lavinia wasn't an animal person. She'd never harm them but she'd never want one, wouldn't want the mess or the commitment but those two were very pretty little dogs as they trotted along in their jewel encrusted collars and pink coats, Lucy and Lady, feathery tails and ears blowing in the gentle wind. They crossed over to her side of the road and stopped to chat.

"Hi darling," breezed Gervais in his breathy voice. "Everybody's out having a tidy up today. Have to spy your chance when it's not piddling down with rain don't you."

"You certainly do! Everything has turned to mush and I wanted to make a bit of a start. I'm not doing too much and trying not to disturb hibernating insects but it all looks such a mess doesn't it."

"Ooh yes it does and I hate mess don't I Gav, so do you don't you."

"I like it to be tidy yes."

Gavin was about ten years older than Gervais Lavinia would guess and seemed quite indulgent of his flamboyant partner. Gervais was Lavinia's hairdresser; she'd been going to his salon, Snippet, in Hartford for some years – word had it that that was how he and Gavin had met, Gavin had been a client, many years ago. Now in their fifties and sixties respectively they shared a close bond that Lavinia envied.

"I suppose we ought to have a go at ours Gav, what do you think?"

"See how we feel later, I don't want to push it with the old – new – hip!"

"Has it all settled in now?" Lavinia asked him.

"Pretty much yes thanks. Quite a long recovery period but Gervais was a good nurse doing everything for me. Great to be pain free though."

"I knew someone who had problems with their hip replacement."

"Yes I believe some do but I've been one of the lucky ones and it's all fine. There's a lot to remember at first, you can't cross your legs, can't drive for six weeks and best not even be a passenger in a car because of the movement, toilet visits are a tricky manoeuvre! Things you wouldn't think about like bending too far forward. It's been well worth it though. I'd recommend it to anyone even though you take your chance. It's given me a new lease of life."

"Are you still doing your paintings?"

"I've usually got a commission or two on the go and we like to go to exhibitions when we can get to them."

"And your students?"

"Yes, classes still ticking over in my garden studio. Same with your flowers?"

"Yes thanks. We all seem to have recovered after the pandemic don't we. Are you back to normal Gervais?"

"Busier than ever darling! It's hard to remember what a difficult time it was for all of us isn't it. Not that long ago but you soon forget the social distancing, the hand sanitizing, having to wear vizors and masks all day when we first came out of lockdown. So uncomfy wasn't it." He waved his arms about in his characteristic style as if flapping with an imaginary flock of birds. He was such a likeable character; everybody loved Gervais. Lavinia hadn't known him in his younger days but people said he'd adored his red patent stilettos and frilly white shirts. Now in his fifties he'd toned down to flat shoes but still loved his buckles and bows. He always looked smart and crisp even now in casual wear, still dyed his hair blond – told everyone he was glad he still had hair to dye! Gavin on the other hand had allowed his grey to grow in naturally and looked very distinguished, Gervais keeping his style neat and tidy for him.

The dogs were getting impatient and eager to be off on their walk so they said their goodbyes and continued on their way. Lavinia watched them go, envious of their closeness. Would she ever have that she wondered?

CHAPTER 46

Willows Dip and its surrounding areas had a good number of literary events. In the main town of Hartford there was a creative writing class in the city library which had spawned several authors and writers. It ran competitions, had literary dignitaries presenting prizes and certificates, produced an annual magazine and held recital evenings.

In the village hall there was a monthly book club. A cosy, informal get together of book fans of all ages where a particular book from their list was read and discussed each month. The conversation usually veered off into other directions but it was a friendly occasion looked forward to by regulars and always welcoming to newcomers.

The village's two most well known authors were Celia Wainwright and Tess Barker. Both had had their lucky break some years earlier and made a comfortable living. For Celia it had been a life saver after she'd become ill with M.E/C.F.S following her divorce and had to take early retirement from her job as a teacher in a special educational needs school, a life shattering event but she'd survived and bought her pretty cottage in Mill Lane. For Tess it had also come following her divorce but she'd been luckier in her health. Her property treat had been her modern four bedroomed detached house in Earls Close, a small cul de sac off Regent Grove; it had become her sanctuary, a balm to her soul with the summer house in the back garden her writing retreat that she and her then gardener Billy Marshall had built before they'd subsequently got together as a couple.

Today Celia was hosting a book signing event at PageTurners bookshop in the neighbouring village of Lower Hayfields, a pretty village favoured by tourists. The marketing had been done and she hoped a good number of her readers would be passing through. She looked at these events with a mixture of pleasure and trepidation – the pleasure because she enjoyed meeting readers and it was always a joy to get feedback on her previous work, trepidation because she never knew if her health was going to play along. Her body was a peevish child; it toyed with her. She'd have a decent day where she felt almost well and was able to go for a short walk with Charles Lewis, her next door neighbour and lover, and she'd feel confident and buoyant, then it would knock her down with its boxing glove of a crash and say, 'Ha, don't get used to that, I was only jesting with you.' A day or several in the recliner chair would follow, aching from head to toe with crushing fatigue and brain fog. She'd learned to manage it over the years after a fashion but it always had the upper hand. She was relieved therefore when she'd done an occasion or event and could look back at the enjoyment.

Charles had come along with her, had done the driving which was a tremendous help to her, and helped her set up her book display. Her handsome Charles with his neat grey hair and beard, she'd never expected him to come into her life when he had but she thanked the angels every day. She always remembered her thoughts when he'd knocked on her door with her not looking her best, she never had fit blokes knocking on her door, but knock he had and on the door to her heart.

Ella Hetherington who worked there showed them to the area set aside for them and helped make Celia comfortable whilst Charles had a look around. Bookworm Ella was interested in the book Celia was promoting, her latest publication entitled A Home for a Ghost. The inspiration had come to Celia following a fire in a 17th Century farmhouse in Little Acorn Lane, Willows Dip some years earlier. Many of the locals had watched in shock as the iconic building had gone up in flames and it was with great sadness that they speculated the cause. The media being the media only what they wanted known was published and nobody knew the truth but the building was said to be haunted and Celia wondered about all of the homeless ghosts. Would they haunt the fields or seek shelter in nearby buildings? Did ghosts need shelter? She could certainly get a story out of that.

It was early afternoon, Celia didn't function before the magic hour of twelve and the small bookshop was doing its usual brisk trade, with added visitors who'd come specially to see Celia and sales were going well.

Ella noticed the dark haired young man the moment he walked in. He it seemed, noticed her simultaneously and approached her with an attractive smile.

"Hi, I'm looking for a book on bees. My mum found one in the bathroom the other day but we thought it was a bit early being February. It was a warm day so perhaps it had got a bit confused."

She returned his smile, totally bowled over by how good looking he was, but it was more than that, she felt drawn to him in just those first few moments. "Sure, over here."

Her blonde ponytail swinging before him as he followed, she led the way to the wildlife section. "There's a good selection here. I think you'll find something suitable. If you need any help just give me a shout."

He looked disappointed as she made to move away. "Oh, aren't you going to look with me?" He peered at her name badge. "Ella. I'm Leo by the way."

That glow that she'd felt initially ignited to a flame and warmed her soul. In these first few moments she wanted to be near this boy and if it took forever to choose the book that wouldn't be long enough. Smiling up at him she replied, "I will if you like. Let's see what we've got."

She drew a book from the shelf and flicked through the pages before handing it to him.

"How about this?"

Their fingers brushed and that flame engulfed her senses like an inferno. How was it possible to feel like this about someone you'd only just met? Five minutes ago she hadn't known of his existence as he'd walked along the street towards the shop and she'd been getting Celia settled. Now her world had taken on this rosy hue and everywhere was pink and gold and light and all because of Leo.

Leo. Leo. Leo.

She handed him another book. He took it, looking into her face with smiling dark eyes. For as long as she lived she wanted to see that smile. How could she keep him here? How could she hold onto him? It was unthinkable that she should let him walk out of this shop now without establishing some form of contact but she couldn't ask him for his number, you just didn't, it would look desperate.

He made his selection. "This one I think. It seems to say a lot about wild bees. I've googled it but there's nothing like a book is there."

"No there isn't. I go to a book club in Willows Dip. It's a good evening's chat about whichever book we've read."

"Sounds good. I might give it a look. Can I have your number and you can tell me more about it?"

They exchanged numbers and Ella wrapped his book for him.

"Great to meet you Ella," he said as he left. "I'll text you later."

Oh happy happy day! How Ella got through the rest of it she

didn't know. She was aware somewhere on the edge of her consciousness of the throng of people surrounding Celia but it didn't register as a thought that the book was being well received. It all passed in a haze of fuzzy, rosy warmth and as she sat eating her tea later both Mum Caitlin and Dad Adam commented on her inner glow.

"I could warm my hands on your cheeks," Adam said at the dreamlike state of his daughter's demeanour. "What's brightened your day?"

Ella gave a breathy sigh. "This most gorgeous boy came into the shop. Leo his name is. He bought a book about bees."

"He's certainly given you a buzz! Sorry," giggled Caitlin, "couldn't resist that one. What's he like?"

"Tall, dark hair and eyes, the most beautiful smile."

"Ah young love, I remember it well, the fluttery heart, the butterflies in your stomach. Eat your dinner though before it gets cold. You'll need to keep your strength up if a new romance is on the cards."

Leo had felt the same impact from their meeting. As he left the shop and walked down the street he couldn't believe what had just happened. He'd walked in to purchase a book, and walked out minus a piece of his heart.

Ella. Her name was like honey from the bee he'd been seeking information on. Forever she would be his little bee.

CHAPTER 47

Ella met Leo outside The Singing Kettle to go to the book club at 7 p.m. They didn't want to meet right outside the village hall where it was held to be obvious to the other members who'd be arriving. They'd texted each other the previous week since their meeting so they'd had a bit of getting to know you chat. He was eighteen, had an elder brother and sister, Ashley and Georgia; he worked as an apprentice electrician. She'd told him she was studying A Level English literature, had two half brothers, Jake and Josh – well Josh wasn't strictly, it was a little complicated – from her dad's first marriage, and a half sister Saba from her mum's. As they crossed the road to the village hall he took her hand and sent delicious tingles all up her arm. He dropped it to hold the door open for her.

As the other members arrived Ella introduced Leo and said he'd come into the shop to purchase a book the previous week. She tried not to notice the knowing smiles especially those of the older romantic novelists, Tess Barker and Celia Wainwright, she wondered if their meeting might end up in one of their books!

The book they were discussing was The Tattooist of Auschwitz by Heather Morris. Leo had read it some time ago so knew the story of Lale Sokolov's memoirs. The moving love story between Lale and Gita amid the sheer horror of all they endured in the death camp was covered and the terrible sights they must have seen. People must have suffered what is now known as PTSD for the rest of their lives.

When the meeting ended at 8.30 p.m. Leo suggested to Ella that they go down the lane to The Seven Stars for a drink.

"Have you driven here?" he asked her.

"I have. Even though it's not far for me to walk it's safer to drive in the dark."

"Agreed. Shall we walk from here to the pub and leave our cars parked here?"

"Yes, good idea."

Once out of sight of the village hall and into the blanketing darkness of the lane he took her hand again.

"What did you think of the evening?" she asked. "Did you enjoy it?"

"I did yes thanks, all the better for you being there of course, my little bee." He squeezed her hand.

She laughed. "Your little bee?"

"The book. I'll always think of you as my little bee, warm and fluffy."

"Ha ha that's nice. I can think of much worse things to be thought of than a little bee. Did you like the book?"

"Yes it's very good. Lots to learn about bees. There are white tailed and red tailed bumble bees, solitary bees, mason bees, all different kinds. I'll definitely be on the lookout for them when spring comes."

"Have you seen any more since the one in your bathroom?"

"No. We think it must have been a queen come out of hibernation early with the odd warm day and was looking for somewhere to nest. We just hoped she went back to hibernate until it warms up properly."

They reached the pub and entered into its warmth and light and were greeted by a buzz of conversation.

"What would you like to drink?" he asked.

"I'll have a coke please."

"Crisps or anything?"

"Ready salted please."

He gave their order to the bartender, got their drinks and they carried them over to a table by the roaring log burner. They sat comfortably together, but she was acutely aware of his muscular thighs pressed up to hers looking so inviting in his snug fitting trousers and she felt an almost uncontrollable urge to squeeze them, then he said, "Tell me about your family. You said Josh was complicated."

"Yes," she replied drawing her eyes away from his thighs, "Josh is complicated. My half brother, or so I grew up believing. My world was shattered when I found out he was no blood relation to me at all. We were so close, both sensitive souls, I thought we'd inherited it from our father – Adam – but then it turned out he isn't Josh's father, Nathaniel is."

"How did that come about? You finding out?"

"It wasn't a sit-down-we've-got-something-to-tell-you moment. Dad just said it matter of factly when we were looking at family photos. I'd said to Dad how Josh and I looked alike, both had his blonde hair and he said it was a coincidence. Josh probably got his hair colour from his mother Chloe. I said it could have been either of them and he said very carefully, I'll never forget it, 'No sweetheart, I'm not Josh's biological father.' The hurt in his eyes left me in no doubt that he was telling the truth but I still had to ask him, 'How can you be sure?' 'We had a DNA test many years ago, Nathaniel's insistence,' he said. 'I'd have been happy believing he was mine but he wanted to know if he was his, I suppose quite rightly. I'd have wanted to know in his position.' I asked him how

Josh felt when he knew and he said his world had crumbled; he'd hated Chloe and Nathaniel, had wanted to come and live with us but Dad reassured him he'd always be his dad even if not his father biologically and he should stick it out at home. I said that Josh and I were always so similar in temperament though but Dad said it was because we'd spent so much time together. I'm also close to Jake and he is my half brother, closer to both of the boys than to Saba, my half sister. We don't see much of her, she's busy with her own life, moved away, she's quite selfish, we never really got on. I wonder if she's like her father. I never knew him. Mum never speaks of him. Anyway let's talk of something a little less heavy. What books did you read as a child?"

"I loved the Harry potter books did you? They were Ashley's being the eldest but both Georgia and I read them."

"Yes I did. Mine were from Jake. What about the Goosebumps books? Did you read those? Again mine were from Jake. I was always going through his books."

"Same, mine were from Ashley. I can't remember the titles though there were so many. What was your favourite Harry Potter? Mine was The Goblet of Fire."

"The Order of The Phoenix, but I loved them all. I wanted to be Hermione but I wouldn't have had her guts."

"Ha ha, nobody I wanted to be, certainly not Malfoy!"

They both laughed then their look became serious as their eyes met.

"Shall we go?" he suggested.

She nodded.

Once outside in the chill night air and the shelter of the bushes surrounding the car park he did what they'd both been wanting all night, took her in his arms and kissed her. A soft, gentle kiss, a hello, getting-to-know-you kiss but both kept it going for long moments before drawing apart, smiling into each other's faces, arms encircling each other as they began to walk back to the village and their cars. They were hardly aware of the slight drizzle falling, dampening their hair, all they were conscious of was the feel of each other's bodies, so warm, so close, and both wanted to stay like that forever.

"Where's your car?" he asked.

"Over there, the Mini."

He walked her to it and kissed her again.

"It's been a wonderful night," she said as they broke off. "Thank you for the drink and crisps."

"Pleasure. There's a nice Italian restaurant the other side of Hartford, shall we go one evening?"

"I'd love to, thank you."

"I'll text you and we'll fix it up."

He kissed her again, long and lingering, making her bones melt.

"Goodnight my little bee. Drive carefully."

CHAPTER 48

The knit and natter ladies were sitting in the back of the church, needles clicking away, chatting about grandchildren and great grandchildren and how they were looking forward to their Easter egg hunts around the village and in their own gardens. The items being knitted were little covers to fit over Cadbury's crème eggs to give out to all the children on Easter Sunday, and flowers to decorate the cross. In addition to the knitted flowers Lavinia was going to decorate it with real flowers, so with them all it should look quite spectacular. The knit and natter ladies were knitting red roses to symbolize the spilt blood of Jesus and white for purity. Lavinia would use what was in season. She discussed it with Steve standing in front of the cross.

I'd thought all spring flowers: daffodils, tulips, primulas. There'll be a variety of colour and the ladies can mingle theirs among them. What do you think?"

"As always I bow to your greater knowledge. It all sounds good to me."

"I can add greenery from ivy and other evergreens to give it backing. Do you want them twisting around it or laid on the front?"

"Oh I think twisting around don't you?"

"Yes it would give it more dimension wouldn't it."

"It would. Let's go in the vestry and grab a coffee, I've had an early start this morning."

He boiled the kettle and produced a packet of chocolate digestive biscuits from the cupboard then took their drinks over to where Lavinia sat at the table.

"My favourite time of year Easter," he said.

"I always like it but I suspect yours is more to do with Jesus than mine. I just like spring and the flowers, the lighter nights and a bit of warmth, although it hasn't been has it."

"No, freezing, perpetual winter! Yes it is mainly Jesus for me but your reasons too."

"Soon be holiday season as well."

"Do you go away much?" he asked sipping the hot drink.

"Not much. I might go with family for a few days if they ask me but I don't invite myself, I'd feel a bit intrusive. Do you?"

"Occasionally I have a mini break but not abroad or anything. You're still dreaming of your island in the Spanish seas then?"

She grinned. "Yes I suppose so, we have our dreams don't we."

There was a lull in conversation as they bit into their biscuits, then he said, "Can I ask you about your divorce?"

"If you really want to know."

"I do."

"Can I ask you about yours?"

"If you really want to know."

"I do."

"Touché."

"OK I'll go first shall I. He was a lying, cheating scumbag, couldn't keep it in his trousers."

"How long were you married?"

"Too long. Eight years but we were together for longer."

"How did you meet?"

"In a pub."

"Did you fancy him straight away?"

"It wasn't a 'wow' moment but he had the chat and he was quite funny."

"Was he good looking?"

"Fairly. Blond, blue eyed, dressed well."

"How long were you together before you married?"

"Four years. I lost track a bit thinking back."

"When did the cheating start?"

"Before then. We were sharing a flat and I suspected he was seeing someone from work. He denied it at first but I saw them together and confronted them. Massive row and I told him we were done. He followed me home, begged forgiveness, swore it was me he loved and he'd never do it again, said she meant nothing and asked me to marry him. Like a fool I said yes, believing every word dripping from his lying tongue. I was young and naïve and thought once the rings were on we'd be safe. How wrong I was."

"When did he cheat again."

"Oh not long after we were married. He was always flirting with some woman all the time we were together, simpering over women, fawning over them, couldn't help himself. I stuck it as long as I could until I could build my business and be self sufficient then I filed for divorce. I got a flat and I was OK, happier than I'd been in ages, free of him. I wasn't always looking for signs all the time, it was refreshing. We'd got a house by then which we sold and split fifty fifty, then my nan died and left me some money so I put a good deposit on where I am now. That's about it. Your turn now. Same questions."

"Similar answers. She wasn't a serial cheat like that, just the once, someone from work but she loved him more than she loved me. Perhaps he was more exciting. Perhaps being the wife of a vicar had been a bit dull. Maybe it was his authority. He was a director of the electrical company she worked for. The suit and tie must have had more of an allure than the dog collar."

He shrugged his shoulders and Lavinia thought that the dog collar was pretty well alluring to her!

"Are they still together?"

"Yes. She upped and left us all. The boys were in their teens and she said it was unfair to disrupt their lives – as if their mother leaving wasn't disrupting their lives! He's got no children. My guess is he wouldn't want them around. He wanted her to himself. If you ask me he's a bit of a control freak but she thinks she's happy. Anyway I was relieved she didn't want to take the boys. She was right that it would have disrupted their lives and I'd have been devastated to lose them as well as her."

"Did you – do you – feel bitter?"

"I did. It tested my faith but you get on with life don't you."

"Has it put you off? You know, ever getting involved again?" She stopped short, wondering if it had come out as a bit of a leading question, as if she was asking for herself.

He in his turn was careful how he answered. "I don't know how to answer that. I could never go through what I went through before, but where do you draw the line at denying yourself the chance of happiness? What about you? Would you ever trust anyone else?"

"For a long time I'd said no but you never know what life holds do you. Of late I've tended to be more open minded."

"Another sensitive subject and don't answer if you don't want to, did you never want children?"

"Not with him. I couldn't trust him and time has passed and I'm too old but I've got my nieces and nephews and we're close so I have experiences of children in my life. I've never known the pain and joy of pregnancy and childbirth but millions haven't have they, just the way it goes."

"Are you happy now?"

"I don't know. Are you?"

"I don't know."

She sighed. "Ah well, such is life."

Steve stood up and collected the cups to rinse in the sink. "Yes," he replied. "We'd better get back out there or the knit and natter ladies will wonder what we're up to."

He gave her a wink as he held the door open for her to go through.

CHAPTER 49

Ella was looking out of the lounge window of their Tudor style four bedroomed detached on the Beechwood estate waiting for Leo to pick her up. He arrived on the dot of 7.30 p.m. peeping the horn of his white Ford Focus. She gave him a wave and skipped past her parents who were trying their best to be discreet in their nosiness and not doing very well.

"Don't we get a look at him?" asked Adam.

She patted his cheek. "Not yet. Too early. Maybe soon."

Caitlin made a supreme effort to wind her giraffe neck in from the window. "He looks nice from what I can see."

Ella laughed. "Mum you can hardly see anything!"

"Well you can't blame me for looking." She refrained from giving her daughter a squeeze so as not to knock a hair out of place. "Have a good time."

"We will."

She almost skipped out of the house and along the path to the car, she couldn't get to him fast enough. He got out to open the door for her, both aware of her parents not-so-well-disguised eyes on them. He held back on the kiss of greeting, didn't want to give them too much of a show.

They chatted about their day as they drove to the restaurant, he holding her hand once the car was cruising in top gear. It was a college day for her, he was working on a refit of a shop not too far away. When they arrived he parked on the car park opposite and they joined hands to cross the road and enter the premises. They were shown to their table and presented with menus.

"What would you like?" he asked after they'd studied them for a while.

"Cannelloni please. What are you going to have?"

"I think I'll have the lasagne. What do you want to drink?"

"I'll have a J20 orange please."

He gave their order to the waiter, adding a pint of lager for himself, then he reached across the table for her hands.

"So you're studying A Level English. Has English always been your favourite subject?"

"Yes, I always loved reading and writing stories. I liked art as well, drawing and painting but I was always better with words. What was your favourite subject?"

"Science, physics. I always wanted to know how things worked. I suppose that's how I ended up training to be an electrician although perhaps a slightly different field."

"It's dangerous though isn't it."

"Life is dangerous isn't it. You just have to watch what you're doing and respect whatever it is you're dealing with."

All the while he was speaking his thumb and fingers were making little whorls on her hands which were quite disturbing in an utterly sensual manner. Her thumbs and fingers had also taken on a will of their own and were performing this intimate dance whilst their voices spoke of every day matters.

"Are you super well read then?" he continued. "Read all the classics?"

"Not all, I don't like everything. I think Emily Bronte's Wuthering Heights has to be one of my favourites."

"The brooding Heathcliff."

"He was very cruel but you could see why from how he'd been treated."

"What drew you to it?"

"Cathy's ghost."

"Do you like a ghost story?"

"Sometimes. Do you?"

"Sometimes. Ah, here's the food."

They dropped hands and concentrated on the serious business of eating.

"This looks delicious. I'm starving!" he exclaimed. "Haven't eaten since lunch, have you?"

"Just a biscuit as I was getting ready. Was it a rush for you?"

"Not too bad. You?"

"No I got back at five so I had plenty of time to make myself presentable."

"You look beautiful." He looked up from his meal, his dark eyes softening, and gave her that smile that melted her heart.

She returned the look. "Thank you and you look very handsome."

Their eyes held for magical moments until they got back to their food. For Ella he was the only boy she'd ever felt such a powerful pull towards. She'd been on casual dates before, practised kisses, fought off groping hands, but nobody had been special; she'd never felt a connection with anybody, until now. Leo was like no-one she'd ever met before. She'd felt it as soon as she'd seen him walk into the shop. Something drew them together, some invisible pull like a thread on a soul level and all she wanted was to be with him. It didn't matter where. Whether it was this lavish meal or a cone of chips walking in town. Being with him was what was important to her and she was overwhelmed by the strength of feeling. She only hoped he felt it too. Surely he must or they wouldn't be here.

They finished their first course and the waiter brought the dessert menu.

"What do you fancy?" asked Leo.

She wanted to say, 'You and only you,' but she answered with, "The banana split looks good. What about you?"

"Same."

He ordered two when the waiter returned.

"Do you want another drink, or coffee?" he asked her.

"No I'm fine thanks, I'm full. Do you?"

"No. We'll have this then go shall we?"

The banana split arrived with a selection of other fruits: kiwi, grapes, ice cream, and was a sweet, light round off to their meal. He paid the bill then they left and headed back to the car, hand in hand.

"Thank you for a lovely meal and a brilliant evening," she said.

He put his arm round her shoulders pulling her close. "It's not over yet."

On the drive back he pulled into a secluded country lane and killed the engine and they did what they'd wanted to all evening, fell into each other's arms. Neither made the first move it was simultaneous, a fluid movement to mould together. The time for talking was done. Now it was time for their bodies to speak their own language and she couldn't get enough of him. His hands were hands she'd never fight off and her skin tingled everywhere he touched setting her very soul aflame. She never wanted these moments to end and she wanted to remain locked in his arms forever. All she was conscious of was his lips on hers, on her cheeks, her neck. The masculine strength of his arms, his hands. She knew she was falling in love with him but was it too soon?

Time lost all meaning until at last he pulled away, took her face in his hands and said, "I'd better get you home. I don't want to get on the wrong side of your dad on our first proper date."

The rest of the drive home was silent except for the radio. She was only conscious of his hand holding hers all the way and she never wanted him to let it go. Pharrell Williams was singing 'Happy' on the radio, and she was, oh so happy. This would be their tune. She turned to glance at Leo as he drove, so strong, so sexy, and he turned his head and gave her that heart skipping smile. "Happy my little bee?"

"I am. So happy." She raised his hand to her lips and kissed it.

CHAPTER 50

Noel was walking back to work after meeting Krystina for lunch when a beggar, homeless person, whatever he was now known as called out to him.

"Spare a couple of quid mate?"

The man was sitting on a sleeping bag in a shop doorway and Noel was surprised his police pal P.C Jack Adams hadn't moved him on.

"I've 'ad no dinner. I just wanted a sausage roll from Greggs," the plea continued.

Noel toyed with the idea of getting him the sausage roll, at least then the money would go on food and not another pipe but he didn't want to get involved. You didn't know someone's story, you didn't know what had brought them to hard times but equally you didn't know who carried a knife. He dug into his pocket and fished out three one pound coins which he dropped onto the man's sleeping bag. The man looked up at him and just for a second their eyes met.

"Cheers mate, you're a gentleman," he said scooping the coins up.

Noel nodded and walked away, a shiver running down his spine. Just in that fleeting glance a memory had stirred from deep within the past, of his mother crying, the hard eyes of his father as he struck her. Those eyes that had looked at him just now.

He looked over his shoulder to see if he was being followed. If his father had recognized him he didn't want him to know where he worked or track him down. Thankfully he wasn't. He was relieved to get back to work out of sight.

All afternoon it was on his mind. Should he tell Krystina? No. She'd want to see him, might feel sorry for him, bring him into their lives. He couldn't allow that, the man was violent. He and his mother had fled secretly and she'd protected them both from him. Now he must protect the woman he loved at all costs.

All through the next week he kept a look out for him, always keeping a distance from where he'd seen him but he never saw him again, that was not on the streets. On the local paper's Facebook post came news of a man of no fixed address being found deceased. No relatives could be traced but the man's name was John Williamson.

Noel had never thought he'd be relieved to hear of someone's death. How else should he feel? He owed the man nothing. Certainly no love or respect. Both had to be earned. Should he be grateful to him for his existence? He couldn't even think that deeply. If they'd stayed with him both he and his mother could have been killed. No, he was nothing to him.

"Any relation of yours?" Krystina asked when she read it.

Noel gave her a lopsided grin. "Not as far as I know."

If she ever saw his birth certificate he'd say John Williamson was a common enough name, besides, this news item would be history by then.

CHAPTER 51

Phew I'm whacked!" exclaimed Erica returning to the living room after settling Isaac, now two and a half months old, in his cot upstairs. He wasn't the greatest sleeper and if they got a three hour stretch they were lucky. He was still in their room, Harvey had moved into Erica's bed and their relationship was experiencing a slow thaw as they cared for their son together.

"Come and sit down," he said patting the sofa beside him, "I've poured you a glass of wine. Did he go off OK?"

"Eventually. I crept out quietly so as not to disturb him." She adjusted the baby monitor on the coffee table in front of them, and took the wine glass Harvey offered, taking a sip. "Hmm lovely, just what I needed."

He'd got a bottle of lager for himself and they sat to choose a film. "Anything particular you want to watch?" he asked.

"I don't mind. I'm so tired I'll probably fall asleep anyway."

"Nothing I'm bothered about either. Shall we have music?"

"OK."

He called to Alexa to play their playlist and grinned. "I always think it's funny that that thing has the same name as your mother."

She chuckled back at him. "I know it is isn't it."

They were both a little drowsy from lack of sleep and the alcohol added to their soporific state. He put an arm around her shoulder and pulled her to him. "I'm sorry I've been such an arse to you throughout your pregnancy."

It was the first time he'd ever put anything into words and she didn't know how to answer. She couldn't say it's OK because it wasn't. He'd put her through hell and she'd faced her pregnancy alone. She didn't know how she'd have coped without her family and friends, but she didn't want to reprimand him and jeopardize the closeness that was creeping back between them.

He continued. "I don't know what happened to me, I think I was scared but I know that's of no help to you. You must have been scared as well and you had the physical aspect to go through. Maybe that made it better, or maybe it made it worse, I don't know." He took a slug of his lager from the bottle. "I'd like to say I wish we could turn the clock back and I'd be different but I don't know that I would and I wouldn't want to live through that again. I feel better now that Isaac is here. How do you feel? How *did* you feel?"

She sipped her wine and took a breath. "Oh where to start. Shock at being pregnant. Devastated that you didn't love me anymore. Jealous and heartbroken that you preferred Gemma's company to mine."

"There's never been anything between Gemma and I. She's been a good friend and listened to all my worries but nothing romantically."

"That's what she told me at the baby shower which eased my mind a bit. It still hurts though that you went to her with your worries when it should have been me you were confiding in."

"I'm sorry."

She hardly dared ask the next question. "How do you feel now?"

He took her glass and put it and his lager on the coffee table then took her in his arms. "I love you Erica. I don't think I ever stopped loving you. I just think my brain, my emotions, all got muddied up, it was like a quagmire inside me and nothing seemed sure anymore. I didn't feel ready to become a father and it had all been thrust upon us before we'd had a chance to decide on our future, don't you think?"

"Maybe. It was a shock to me too."

He kissed her and they both felt their old feelings flood to the surface. Their kisses became more passionate and they slid to the hearthrug in front of the fire. As twilight gathered the last months of losing each other melted away in arms, hands, lips, legs, bodies as they became one once more. Afterwards she lay with her head on his chest and he caressed her back, kissing the top of her head.

"We can do this parenting thing can't we."

She smiled up into his face. "We can."

CHAPTER 52

Steve had been adding little extras in his prayers to the Lord, prayers of a personal nature. One was for decent weather, at least dry for the Palm Sunday procession round the village. They always had one but this year was extra special, Miranda Montague-Smythe as she was before her marriage, an ex villager, sister of Sebastian, Connie Watson's neighbour and volunteer at the sanctuary in Little Acorn Lane, was bringing one of her donkeys. She had riding stables with her husband in a nearby village and she also kept two donkeys.

"I'll bring Pebbles," she told Steve. "He's a soft pale colour, lovely temperament and is very good with people, adores attention so he'll do the job perfectly and the children will love him. My other donkey, Bramble, darker coloured, is a cantankerous bugger and not averse to having an odd peevish nip at anyone passing. He wouldn't do at all."

"Oh no don't bring Bramble," Steve had laughed. "We don't want any misbehaving from either animals or people!"

His second personal prayer held a note of panic, please let his family keep their big mouths shut and innuendos to themselves around Lavinia. He had had to confront his feelings for her and knew he'd have to make some sort of decision concerning her but how? When? Where did they go from here? Would they have a future together? Would there be marriage? Would she want that? Would *he*?" So many questions. He knew he had strong feelings for her. Was that love? He was afraid of failure but should you take a chance in life? He'd let it drift for all of these months and if he didn't decide soon perhaps she'd get tired of waiting and any feelings she might have for him might fade having gone unnurtured. Such a big step though. What to do, and he certainly didn't want his family pushing the issue with any leading remarks!

The day dawned dry and he offered up a thank you. There was a chilly breeze but he reasoned that you couldn't have everything, he was just thankful that the skies weren't tearful. The congregation gathered in the churchyard, palm crosses were distributed and everyone fell into line behind Steve and Miranda, leading Pebbles.

She'd been right and not only children but adults had adored him and he'd basked in the fuss, soulful dark eyes blinking serenely.

"Give him a piece of carrot," she'd said to two little girls dressed in matching purple warm coats with fur edged hoods, and black patent boots, reminding her of being dressed in her Sunday best as a child for church. "Hold your hand flat like this so that he doesn't catch your fingers with his teeth." She demonstrated to them and their faces beamed as Pebbles' velvet lips brushed their small hands to take the treat.

"He can have some more when we get back," Miranda told the other children so that they all had a turn at giving him a tasty titbit.

As they processed round the village they sang Ride On Ride On In Majesty, a rousing poignant hymn denoting Jesus' short time left on earth before the cruel end that was to come. On returning to church Pebbles was given more carrot treats by the children before being taken home as the service continued inside. The concluding hymn was All Glory Laud and Honour.

Lavinia had her usual seat at the back of the church although she noticed that there were more people attending, several faces that she hadn't seen before. Steve was aware of his sons and their girls on the opposite side and a little further forward than Lavinia and again he sent a silent thank you that they weren't too close. He'd accepted that the best bet was to make formal introductions and he was more nervous about that than he was about the whole service, which had become second nature after all these years. As he ended with, 'Go in peace to love and serve the Lord,' and the congregation had responded, 'In the name of Christ, Amen,' his mouth had gone dry.

People left the church; some went home, some stayed for coffee as usual. Steve mingled, his family hovered with their coffee, as did Lavinia, waiting as she always did for those precious few moments with him. His duty performed, having spoken to those wanting to speak to him, heart hammering, Steve sought out Lavinia. He took her elbow.

"Come and meet my family."

He didn't know whether to be happy or unnerved about the smiles of glee on the faces of his boys and their girls, as he made the introductions.

"Lavinia, this is my family. David, the eldest by half an hour and his partner Grace. Mark and his partner Lucy." Then turning to Lavinia. "This is my friend Lavinia."

A lot of 'Pleased-to-meet-yous,' were exchanged and pleasant smiles and small talk and Steve still didn't relax for fear of what they might say that might be a trifle awkward, then Grace said, "How long have you been friends then?"

Steve and Lavinia looked at each other questioningly and Lavinia was the first to speak, Steve was still on edge.

"I suppose it came about with the death of my next door neighbour. Steve officiated at the funeral and I did the flowers."

"Do you do all the flowers for the church?" asked Mark.

"Not all. It depends who the clients want for funerals, weddings etc, different people choose different florists, but I do them fairly often don't I Steve."

"Yes and a beautiful job. The archway for the wedding a while back was spectacular."

"Thanks. Jess and I did enjoy doing that one. What do you all do?" she asked them.

"I'm a teaching assistant at a primary school," answered Lucy.

"We're both in I.T. Grace and I," David added.

"I'm in the building trade," informed Mark, "a joiner, I love wood, I think I get it from my granddad, Dad's dad, he can turn his hand to anything and once we start talking wood there's no stopping us!"

"It's good though," Steve put it, "I'm pleased you've got something from Dad. It's an interest for him as well now he's getting on a bit."

"Always good to have family bonds," said Lavinia, "but I must go, I left my dinner in the oven and it'll be about ready now. Lovely to meet you all."

"You too," they echoed.

They watched her leave the church and Steve grinned at them, more relaxed now. "Satisfied?"

"Absolutely!" replied David.

"Did you like her? Does she pass inspection?"

"She does yeah, really chatty and pleasant."

"Phew, thank goodness for that."

"Why, are you going to ask her to marry you?"

"Give me a chance, I haven't even asked her out yet!"

"No way! You olds are so slow. You need to hurry up before she runs off with someone else!"

Lavinia meanwhile walked back to her car on air. He'd introduced her to his family! She'd met the kids! He'd made a point of doing so. It wasn't just a casual meeting bumping into them in town, he'd actually taken her over to meet them. Surely that must mean something, mustn't it? You didn't just go introducing people to your family did you?

'Don't go reading too much into it. He said you were his friend, nothing more. It doesn't mean a thing,' said her inner voice. Nevertheless as she put the key in the ignition and started the car she couldn't keep that little zing from her heart!

CHAPTER 53

Easter Sunday dawned sunny but with the ever present chill breeze. Reverend Steven Oswald stood at the door of St Luke's church to welcome his congregation.

The first to arrive were the Simcock sisters, bickering up the church path, Sadie wearing a bright emerald green outfit, and Lydia a more sedate beige.

"See we're not late," Sadie was saying. "I told you we had plenty of time."

"Yeah well you should have started tarting yourself up a bit earlier and we wouldn't have had such a rush. Morning Vicar."

"Morning Lydia, Sadie."

Sadie flashed him a smile. "Morning Vicar."

They moved inside to their normal pew. "The vicar's looking hot in his gold colour," mused Sadie appreciatively.

"Well you can take that stupid look off your face," snapped

Lydia, "I've told you before he's a man of God he'll be wise to your wiles. Besides he's only interested in that woman from the florist's."

Sadie's head shot round. "How do you know that?"

"You can tell by the way they look at each other, it's written all over their faces. The only ones who don't seem to have noticed it are those two themselves."

The church began to fill up and Steve welcomed them all in. The O'Keefes, Chole and Nathaniel with Liliana and boyfriend Ryan, Jade and Josh with baby Marnie in the pram. Jake and Helena and their children joined them sitting in the pew behind. Adam and Caitlin Hetherington behind them with Ella and Leo, now inseparable had gone along too. Ella had been wary of suggesting church to Leo in case he thought she was harbouring dreams of a fairytale wedding but he'd been happy to go along. They had already said that they wanted each other in their future anyway.

Connie, Ellis and Olivia Watson, Jade's father and his family followed stopping off beside the pram to coo to his first granddaughter.

"She's really grown!" said Olivia.

"Certainly has," added her father, "she changes every time I see her."

Erica and Harvey came in with Isaac in the pram along with both sets of parents.

Jade's mother Donna and partner Theo arrived with their friends and neighbours Tess Barker the author and her partner Billy Marshall, gardener to many locals.

"Everything OK for this afternoon at ours?" Donna asked Jade.

"Yes we're all organized thanks. See you about two."

"Not that warm for a barbeque but it'll be a nice family get together."

Theo's family: Saskia and Richie with their three year old daughter Ivy Evelyn, and his son Ross and Josie with their daughter Summer Lily, were also going for the barbeque. The little girls were only a month apart in age, borderline lockdown babies, and thus were devoted to each other.

"The girls can't wait to see Marnie," Donna continued. "They want to know if they'll be able to push her in the pram."

Jade smiled that proud maternal smile. "I'm sure that can be arranged. A short walk along the grove would be good for them."

More people arrived and the pews were getting full so Sue the verger brought chairs out to line up along the back of the church as Noel and Krystina walked in, closely followed by Celia Wainwright, the village's other author with Charles Lewis. The young Australian family who lived over the common arrived, Todd, Ria and their daughter Alicia Rose, who went to sit next to Noel as she knew him from walking with Snowball her cat when Noel walked Macy his dog. Also coming along for the Easter service were the village police officers, Jack Adams and Lacey Miller with their families. Everyone was out for this special Christian festival. Everyone except Lavinia.

Steve was beginning to get worried. Where was she? She was usually fairly early so as to get her regular seat. He hoped nothing had happened to her. Surely she wouldn't just decide against coming if there wasn't a reason. It was such a big event in the church calendar and he'd really wanted her there, then just as he was thinking he'd have to close the door and begin the service there she was, hurrying along the road and his heart soared. She came rushing up the path all breathless and dishevelled and looking utterly desirable and he wanted to hug her and squeeze her tight.

"Couldn't get parked," she gasped clutching her side. "Running late. What a morning. Hair straighteners broke hence the wild look." She flicked her hair up with her fingers.

"Looks just fine to me," he said appreciatively. "Come on, let's go in."

From the front of the church he began the service.

"The Lord be with you."

"And also with you."

"Lift up your hearts."

"We lift them to the Lord."

Lavinia sat trying to get her breath back and selected the first hymn from the hymn book, Jesus Christ is Risen Today. As she sang she thought how much more uplifting it was than the Good Friday service. She hadn't enjoyed that at all. It had taken place on a hill at the edge of the common where three crosses had been erected and whilst having had a Christian upbringing and knowing the story off by heart it was the first time she'd been to this particular service and it had never seemed more poignant and heartbreaking. To see those three crosses there made it all so real, the enormity of it, the horror of it. How could God have let it happen?

The hymn ended and she realized she'd sung it on autopilot whilst contrasting it to Friday. The service progressed as usual but took longer by the sheer volume of people. The queue in the aisle to go for Holy Communion or to be blessed seemed never to end but at last it was her turn and as always she treasured these few brief moments between her and Steve. It looked like they'd be all she'd get this week with so many people all clamouring for his attention afterwards; she'd never get near him.

She was proved right as people stayed for coffee and biscuits and to chat and no-one seemed in any rush to leave.

'Go home!' she thought – and to God, 'Please make them go! *I* want him. He's *mine*!'

However God didn't seem to be listening. She made polite conversation with everyone else, she couldn't think what about, inane chat, it meant nothing when the man she wanted was surrounded like a rockstar by throngs of adoring fans.

For the millionth time she thought, 'Oh just give up,' put down her coffee cup and left quietly and unnoticed – well not quite unnoticed – Steve just caught a glimpse of her retreating back and was as disappointed as she was.

She dragged herself slowly, despondently, back to her car on feet of lead. She unlocked the door but somehow couldn't bring herself to get in, she just stood staring at her distorted reflection in the window. After what seemed like an age she locked the door again; she just couldn't leave without telling Steve how she felt about Good Friday. Turning, she headed back to the church.

Miraculously the crowds had gone and just the last few people were drifting down the church path. The door was closed. Carefully she turned the heavy ringed handle and it creaked as she pushed it open. Steve was in there alone extinguishing the candles, the smell of hot wax, that church smell hanging heavy on the air as tendrils of smoke spiralled upwards from each one. He turned when he heard the door and his face lit up with a smile.

"Lavinia! I thought you'd gone."

"I had to come back and tell you about Good Friday."

"What about it?"

They were at the front of the church now by the front pews which faced the lectern. He sat down. She remained standing, facing him.

"I just found it so moving, so sad, poignant, thoroughly heartbreaking."

"Haven't you felt that before?"

"Not so powerfully. I've watched films about the crucifixion and they've made me cry but I think seeing those three crosses just made it so real. Does it get you like that?"

"It does yes but we know why don't we."

"I just think it's so cruel. When Jesus said, 'Take this cup from me.' There must have been another way. How could God do it?"

A tear rolled down her cheek and he held a hand out to her. "Come and sit by me."

She took his hand and did so. His hand was warm and firm, just as she knew it would be and he didn't let go but looked into her eyes. "Another way wouldn't have had the impact would it."

She shook her head and looked at him through a haze of tears. She was lost in his eyes, their dark depths, their gentleness drawing her in, then he released her hand, took her face in his hands, brushed the tears from her cheeks with his thumbs and kissed her. It was the sweetest, gentlest kiss she'd ever had and the one she'd waited all her life for and she never wanted it to end. As she was drowning in his kiss a tiny thought shimmered in the recesses of her mind. Perhaps tea on the lawn with the old dears would be quite tolerable if it meant sharing her life with this wonderful man.

The Willows Dip Series

Each book is a separate story and will stand alone but Book Two, After the Solstice is sequel to Book One, A Lapse of Sanity, other than that all stories are different with new main characters but with earlier characters making an appearance around the village, an update on their lives, and how they interact with new characters.

The Hetheringtons and O'Keefes are the original characters from Books One and Two, A Lapse of Sanity and After the Solstice.

The Watsons and Little Acorn Bird Sanctuary are the feature of Book Three Free Flight. Book Four A Treasure Lost is a murder mystery surrounding the Hetheringtons, O'Keefes and Watsons.

Book Five Not Reported Missing introduces a new character, an author, Celia Wainwright who moves into Connie Watson's nana's cottage. This book also introduces characters who live on the outskirts of Willows Dip in a select cul de sac called Regent Grove, Jade Watson's mother Donna, who features in the book, Whisper to Me, not a part of the series but with a link towards the end. This book features Theo Stanyer's story. Other characters introduced in Not Reported Missing from books outside the series but living in Regent Grove are Tess Barker and Billy Marshall, their story is in the stand alone novel The Author, The Gardener and The Woman What Does, and the characters from the two Over a Spitfire books. In the concluding chapters of Not Reported Missing a new family arrives from Australia, fleeing the bush fires at the end of 2019, and just at the outbreak of the coronavirus Covid 19, Todd, Ria and Alicia Rose.

Book Six Don't Cough on Me was never intended to be written but then along came Covid 19, the global pandemic and its effect on Willows Dip had to be explored. It features the experiences of all villagers and how the virus affected their lives.

Neighbourhood Watching was a bit of fun for the author, imagining the nosiness among the villagers as they speculated on each other's lives, often getting the wrong end of the stick. Thus, a collection of short stories was born. In this collection, two stories, God Works in Mysterious Ways, and All That Hand Washing For Nothing, sparked the idea for Book Seven, Soul Saver. The Reverend Steven Oswald had first appeared as a minor character some twenty years earlier in A Lapse of Sanity, so it was about time he had his own story.

Book Eight is in the planning stages, notes in notepads, a little bit of research done but will possibly centre around a relocation to a beautiful island for a new character connected to a minor one in Book Seven, with updates on all of the regulars and developments from the concluding chapters of Soul Saver. Watch this space!

All can be purchased in ebook format from Amazon and various other platforms and in paperback from feedaread.com

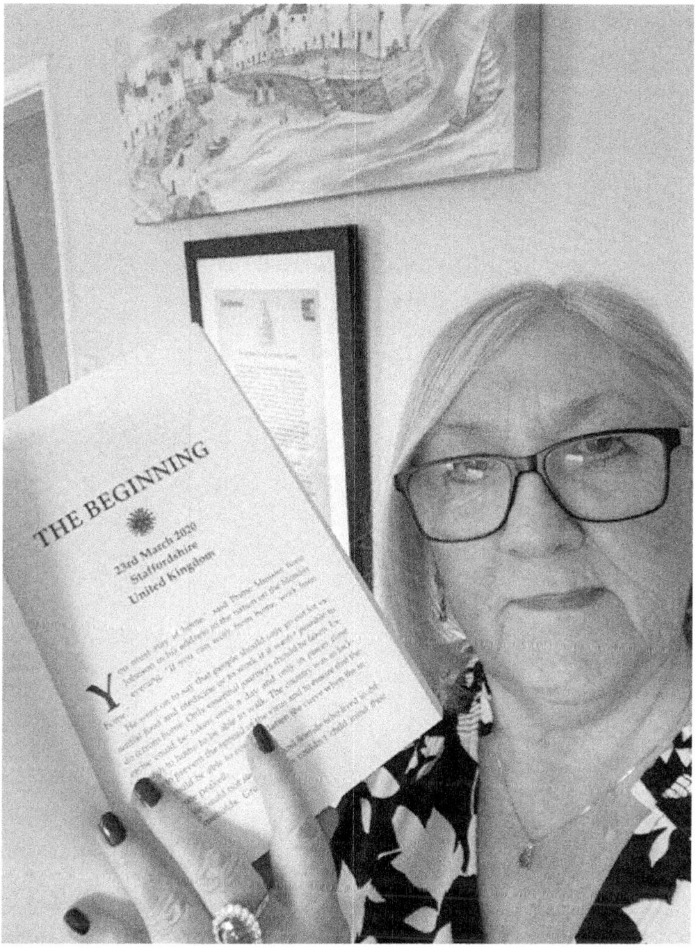

Sherrie Lowe is a divorced mum and nanna living in Staffordshire UK. She began writing seriously when she became ill with M.E in 1995, after having to resign from her job as learning support assistant in a mainstream high school because she was too ill to continue. M.E, also called chronic fatigue syndrome is a little understood, debilitating illness that destroys lives. Writing has kept her sane through the loneliness and isolation that are a part of this condition.

On the positive side she had time on her hands and developed an interest in writing. When she was well enough she attended a creative writing class and learned to write fiction. To date she has published 16 books as memoirs, novels and short story collections.

Visit the author's website:
www.sherrielowe.co.uk

Follow Sherrie Lowe on X:
@SherrieLowe2

Printed in Great Britain
by Amazon

47167821R00128